The Fall of Water House

THE ELEMENTALISTS • BOOK 1

MICHELLE JARVIS

If one day you have to choose between the world and love, remember this: If you choose the world you'll be left without love, but if you choose love, with it you will conquer the world.

— ALBERT EINSTEIN

Contents

One

The Elementalists were coming. Try as she might to forget it, Rosalinde couldn't. She typically looked forward to the yearly feast and the week-long celebration that accompanied it; in fact, her mother had always accused her of enjoying the Elemental Festival a bit *too* much.

But this year was different.

This year, Princess Rosalinde would be participating in the Great Match, rather than simply watching it. She would spend the week with suitors from each of the elemental houses, watching them compete and engaging with them through different activities. At the end of the week she would be engaged to whomever she chose.

Not that there was much choice at all. Her mother wanted her to choose an Earth Elementalist, to bind the queen's familial house ever closer to the throne. Her father, on the other hand, wanted to align with the Fire

Elementalists, believing that any challenge to the throne in the years to come would be from the Air house. He needed to forge ties with the other houses while he could. Her parents had declared themselves as rivals, unbeknownst to one another, but Rosalinde wouldn't tell them that.

Even the thought of the Great Match sent her stomach swirling with anxiety and a very unladylike need to forfeit the few contents of her stomach. Not only would she disappoint one of her parents with whatever choice she made, but it also wasn't likely she would find someone to her liking amongst the snooty nobility she had grown to loathe through the years. Sure, she was royalty herself and accustomed to a life of luxury, but she often had trouble feigning interest in the hobbies and behaviors of the peers from which she was supposed to choose her spouse.

Over the years, she'd met most of the men who would be competing for her hand. Some had been playmates as children, or rivals in the games that the teenagers played during the celebration week. A few had attempted to cement themselves as suitors in the years leading up to Rosalinde's time in the Great Match, either through extravagant gifts or flowery words, both of which held little substance in her opinion. Although those attempts did not make a positive impression, she couldn't say they failed, either. If nothing else, the names of those potential mates were sealed in her mind.

Still, she couldn't recall anyone she had more than a

passing attraction to at best. Most felt more like distant cousins than potential husbands. They were all... fine. There was nothing *wrong* with them, but there also wasn't anything that sparked even the slightest interest in Rosalinde's heart. They were coming to compete for ties to the throne, not for her. Knowing the houses as she did and the many noble families that made them up, how could she ever marry one of those men?

But alas, she must. For now, all she could do was smile and try to enjoy her last moments of freedom before the Great Match began.

Rosalinde turned from the window where she'd been watching street vendors vying for the best spots to set up their stalls. Inside the castle it was just as hectic; servants ran every which way trying to prepare for the mages' arrival, their arms full of food, decorations, wrapped gifts, and small tokens of appreciation to be placed in the visiting nobles' rooms.

As she walked down the halls, Rosalinde studied the varied banners from each house. Though there were only four main houses—Water, Earth, Air, and Fire—each house had many branches, and each branch had a banner on display as she trekked to the dining hall. The whole palace was awash with a myriad of bright colors strung high and low, and she reveled in the beauty of it all.

In addition to the banners clearly woven by a master craftsperson, there were also vast floral displays throughout the castle. Ros stopped more than once to smell the blossoms the Botanical Elementalists had raised from seed to bloom in a matter of seconds. She was always amazed at the work they performed, though she knew they must be the best in the country to be employed by her father, the king.

These were the parts she enjoyed, the small details that made this yearly feast different from those in the past. And part of her *was* looking forward to the week-long celebration that accompanied it, the games and trials and feats of power. The celebration week had always been her favorite part of the year. Not this year though; try as she might, her spirits were in ruin and her brain could not stop cycling through the images of her potential mates, and nothing proved a consistent distraction.

She shivered, attempting to shake off the thoughts as she stepped into the great hall. It would not do to dwell on things she could not change. Instead, she took a deep breath and focused on the things happening around her. The mages who lived and worked in the castle were bustling about, preparing a grand display for the impending festivities, showcasing the talent and vitality of the Water house staff.

Her mother, Queen Sariyah of Talabrih, was on the far end of the great hall near the windows, directing a group of Botanical mages who served at her behest. From a spattering of seeds, the mages raised a miniature forest with an unusual collection of different trees, jade vine and surcuvian moss dangling from them.

As Rosalinde watched, Sariyah lifted her hand in the air and a garden sprouted from the floor. Red hibiscus intermingled with freesia, foxglove and silversword appeared as speckles of blue sapphire orchids, orange mystiques, and tea roses grew alongside one another. There were half a dozen blooms she couldn't name, and several she was certain had been created from her mother's imagination, but all blended into a floral masterpiece.

Her mother was an accomplished mage, one of the strongest that Earth House had ever known, and certainly the greatest Botanical mage of her time. It was this strength that led to her marriage to Rosalinde's father, King Tancred. He was a powerful mage in his own right, a Healer who specialized in blood magic, a rare gift among Water Elementalists.

When her parents had participated in the Great Match twenty-five years ago, it had been her mother battling against thirty-seven of the kingdom's most powerful women to gain *Prince* Tancred's attention. Each of the houses had presented their best, strongest mages in every aspect they could muster. Although the four major houses only provided a mere two dozen common combinations, unlikely pairings would inevitably manifest countless outlying magical powers. These rare gifts were highly favored or grossly detested, depending on who you discussed them with and which house was in favor at the time.

One such rare outlier was Queen Sariyah's fiercest competition: a wielder of shadows and darkness, a Night Elementalist named Ombretta. She wasn't from a noble house, that much she admitted, though she refused to speak of her parentage further. Many guessed at the elemental combination that led to her unusual gift, but Night Elementalists were too rare to know precisely how they came to be. Even in the recorded history of Talabrih, Ombretta was only the second in existence.

It was this fear of the unknown, of who Ombretta was and the mystery surrounding her gift, that ultimately turned Prince Tancred away from the Night House and toward his future wife. The two women were the strongest of the competitors, but all things being equal, the future king preferred a magic he understood. Stories say when he announced his choice, Ombretta dispersed into wisps of shadow that vanished into the night, never to be heard from again.

"Ros darling, what are you doing?" King Tancred put his hand on his daughter's shoulder, spooking her out of her thoughts. "What is troubling you?"

Rosalinde turned to address her father, attempting to smooth her features with a practiced smile. "I'm fine, Father."

Tancred furrowed his brow. "You're sure? Is it something to do with the Match? It's understandable to be nervous."

"No, of course not," Rosalinde said. "I was just lost in my head. You know how I can be."

She wasn't sure if he believed her, but he nodded and let it go. His eyes scanned the room to find his wife. Like most relationships among the upper class, their union wasn't founded on love. Still, Rosalinde knew her parents had grown fond of each other through the years. They didn't have a life of passion, but they had built something solid, a haven to weather life's storms. If they wanted romance, they had lovers for that.

Ros winced at the thought. She wasn't supposed to know about their dalliances, their torrid affairs. But of course she did. It wasn't uncommon for rulers to take lovers, but her parents preferred to keep that part of their lives discreet, taking special care to hide it from their children.

Rosalinde, however, was adept at rooting out secrets —a trait she shared with her younger sister. Ros was ten when she heard the first whisper of one of her mother's lovers slipping away down a side hall. She hadn't quite understood what it meant until she turned thirteen and overheard the maids talking about another tryst.

She'd been horribly disgusted at first, as young people often are at the thought of her parents having lovers. She didn't care if *other* people did; in fact, even young Rosalinde believed in finding love wherever one could, as long as all parties consented. But it wasn't someone out in the world finding a little pleasure—it was her *parents*.

What hit Ros hardest of all was the idea that they didn't love one another. It hurt her to think of them hating their lives and being trapped in them. But as she got older, she came to understand them better. As she learned more about the Great Match and it became an inevitability instead of just a fairytale story the maids would tell when she was eavesdropping, Ros felt more sympathy and gratefulness toward her parents. They weren't trapped in their lives; no, they had chosen to make sacrifices for their kingdom and they would do it a hundred times over if it meant a better home for their people.

"Sometimes I forget how good she is," Tancred whispered, as if to himself.

Ros smiled up at him, at the way he watched Queen Sariyah in awe. She said, "The queen is a master."

"She's a pleasure to watch. Such ease, such grace. I could watch her forever."

"She likes watching you work, too."

It was true. Queen Sariyah's presence in the healing ward was often noticed. She would sweep through the hallways in search of her husband, peeking through windows and cracks in doors to watch him working his healing magic.

Tancred smiled. "She has no idea how the world holds its breath at her very presence."

There was something in his tone that made Rosalinde take notice. Her parents always spoke well of one another, especially in front of Ros and her little sister, Elsabet, but today King Tancred's tone spoke of something else, something deeper. Perhaps his love for his wife was more complicated than Ros realized.

The Botanical mages finished their creations and departed for their other tasks, leaving only Queen Sariyah, and to Ros's surprise, Elsabet. She hadn't noticed her sister among the others, but her presence shouldn't have been unexpected. Though Ros's gift was firmly between Earth and Water, her sister leaned into Earth house. She wasn't as skilled as their mother, but she could be with practice and dedication. Unfortunately, those were two things Elsabet had no interest in.

Ros watched as the two crossed the room toward her and her father. They were so similar, from the tops of their dark wavy heads, down to the perfectly manicured tips of their fingers and toes. Their mother was a little shorter than the sisters, but she walked with a confidence that left Ros awestruck. Both women were lean, waif-like creatures that exuded something almost ethereal. They brought to mind the descriptions of fae royalty from the storybooks Ros loved as a child. They were more than beautiful—they were *perfection*.

Jealousy rose like bile in Ros's throat. She'd always wanted to look like her mother, praying to the elements themselves to let her possess even a small part of Sariyah's beauty. She's spent her youth hoping that she might grow into those looks, becoming more like her mother as she aged. But that never happened. Instead, Ros took after her father. Her hair was red and poker-straight, framing periwinkle eyes and porcelain skin. Her figure was curvy, soft in ways her sister was not.

Ros knew she wasn't unattractive. Plenty of heads turned wherever she went. But she didn't have that mysterious air that surrounded her mother and sister. It was something she was always aware of, no matter who she was speaking to. She might be lovely in her own right, but when Elsa or Sariyah entered the room, everything else stopped. Conversations paused mid-sentence, eyes swiveled to them, and you could practically feel the breath catch of every person nearby. Ros found it... annoying.

Instead of bearing the mystery and intrigue of her mother's side, Rosalinde's round face told all her secrets. She couldn't keep her expression neutral, couldn't hide the thoughts behind her eyes. She practiced in front of the mirror daily, but she couldn't stop her eyes from sparkling when she felt joy, couldn't keep from scrunching her nose when she was disgusted, and her skin flushed red with embarrassment and anger alike.

"Hello, my love," King Tancred said as they reached them. He withdrew Sariyah's seat as she smiled up at him.

"You're in a good mood, Your Highness," Sariyah said.

"Of course," he said, taking his own seat. "I have the pleasure of dining with my favorite people for this fine midday meal, the castle is looking marvelous, thanks to your hard work, and tonight I'll share drinks and stories with friends I haven't seen for a year. What could be finer?"

"Too right, father. The day is certainly bright. And I'm delighted to see that my lovely sister finally made it out of bed to join us." Elsa stretched her arms above her head and gave a fake yawn.

Their mother swatted at Elsa. "Arms down. You're a Princess. Act like it."

"Me?" Elsa asked. "I'm not the one entertaining *guests* all evening and sleeping all morning."

Rosalinde narrowed her eyes at her sister, willing her to shut her mouth. She didn't know how Elsa knew who came and went to her room, but it wasn't a discussion she wanted to have in front of her parents.

"Yes, well, you know how Larkin is, always flitting about at all hours," Ros said.

"Oh, Larkin was here? Why didn't she stop to say hello?" Queen Sariyah asked.

With her lips twisted in a wicked smirk, Elsa said, "That seems so unlike her."

"Isn't her brother competing in the Great Match?" Tancred asked.

Ros was grateful for the subject change. "Indeed, he is."

"He's wasting a spot," Elsa said.

"Why do you say that?" Sariyah asked, leaning around the servant delivering her food.

"He's not the strongest metal worker Earth has to offer, they just think he's got a shot because his sister is best friends with Ros. But there's no way she would pick Lyzandor."

"How do you know who I will or won't choose? Even I don't know yet."

Elsa rolled her eyes. "If you wanted Lyzandor, you'd

have had him already. He's had a thing for you since that jousting match six years ago."

Rosalinde felt heat creeping up her neck, spotting her cheeks and the tips of her ears with color. Before she could respond, their father cut in with a chuckle, "The match where Ros destroyed him?"

Elsa nodded. "After that beating, he never looked at her the same."

"And how would you know how Zandor was looking at anyone?" Ros asked. "Were *your* eyes so transfixed by him?"

Elsa's brows rose. "I was eleven. What else did I have to do but spy on you?"

Tancred laughed at their arguing, but Sariyah tutted at her daughters. "Honestly, can't you two get along for one meal?"

"You're the one always encouraging us to be our true selves," Ros said, but her lips curled in a smile.

Sariyah sighed and cut into the candied turnips on her plate. Though she didn't look up, Ros heard the weight her voice held as she said, "I think Lyzandor would be a fine match, if you saw fit. He's from a lovely family with whom we're already well acquainted. And your marriage would ensure a quality match for Larkin. She would likely be the prize for the Great Match next year."

The prize. The words surged through Ros, alongside a sweeping bout of disgust. She had no desire to be any man's *prize.*

"You can't be serious," Tancred said through a mouthful of cherry-soaked stag. For a moment, Ros thought the words had caused the same effect in him. But then he waved his fork at Elsabet and said, "She's right about this one. He's a fine young man, but he's no match for Ros."

"There's no man alive you'd be happy with where Rosalinde is concerned."

Tancred pursed his lips at Sariyah, but shot a look to Ros that confirmed her mother's statement. She already knew her father wasn't impressed with any of the men in the Great Match; at least, not of the ones he knew about. Even when he'd told her he hoped to align with the Fire Elementalists, there wasn't a single mage he could name who he felt would be his daughter's equal. Still, there were some disciplines who hadn't confirmed their participants, and it was in those that Ros was placing her hope.

Ros looked down at her plate, ignoring the friendly bickering that continued between her parents. The very sight of the food made her stomach somersault. In a few hours, she'd be seated in this same room, surrounded by people she barely knew, and some she didn't want to know.

But there was no way around it: the Elementalists were coming, and with them, Rosalinde's future.

Two

Ros sat on her bed, staring out the open window at the carriages filing down the lane. Pulling the transports were magnificent creatures made from the elements: a molten stallion pulled an obsidian rig; a massive team of oxen forged from the mountains themselves carried a wagon overflowing with gifts of gems and jewels, a pair of Earth Elementalists perched atop them; a phoenix of wind sailed above the road, a dark-haired mage clinging to nothing but air.

They were an exhilarating sight, each new arrival stranger and more elaborate, hoping to catch the attention of those who watched them pass. Those watching, mages and non-magical folks alike, would be talking about their arrivals all evening, choosing favorites to cheer for in the Great Match and the other competitions. As recently as last year, Ros would've been at her window cheering along with them, but today she felt no joy at their arrival, only a sinking feeling that pulled her ever-farther down.

"I'm sorry about earlier," Elsa said.

Ros jumped and turned to see her sister in the doorway. Her voice had been soft, unnaturally so, but it was the look on her face that nearly broke Ros.

She swallowed, tried to push away her sadness. She put on her practiced face, the one she wanted to be royal and mysterious as she tried to emulate her mother and sister. "It's fine."

But it was no use. Elsa could see right through her. She walked to the bed and wrapped her arms around Ros. "It's not. I was trying to get under your skin, but I shouldn't have mentioned seeing Alaric leaving your room. I can't imagine how hard it was for you to say goodbye to him this morning."

Ros grimaced, but didn't say anything. She knew what her sister must be thinking, and she was somewhat right. Alaric was a friend who sometimes warmed her bed, but she wasn't in love with him. He was kind, different from the noble houses because, well, he wasn't noble. He couldn't be. Alaric didn't have any magic.

But it wouldn't matter even if he did. She didn't love him. She wouldn't choose him if she could. Or at least she'd been telling herself that for long enough that she had started to believe it.

Ros leaned into her sister's embrace, smelling the aftereffects of her magic: the scent of honeysuckle clung to her hair, the spicy aroma of dianthus on her skin.

Every Elementalist had their own scent after using magic. Rosalinde's fragrance was salt mixed with the smell of the air right before a storm. The individual works of each Botanical Elementalist in a vast garden would often retain a hint of the creator's distinctive perfume mixed with the flower's natural odor. No matter how many orchids, lilies, or roses their mother created, she still always smelled of peonies.

Before she wanted to, Ros pulled away. There weren't a lot of sweet moments between her and Elsabet. They loved each other, undoubtedly, but their relationship was one of opposites, cool and prickly with only the rarest moments of warmth.

It didn't matter that Rosalinde would have preferred to spend the evening curled up with her sister, enjoying one of those rare warm moments. Ros knew by the evening light that it was time to descend the stairs and meet the guests assembled in the rooms below.

Elsa knew too, and she forced a smile, saying, "Ready, princess?"

The girls stood and smoothed out their dresses. Ros wore a gown the blue of lapis lazuli with a gauzy sleeveless bodice trimmed in tanzanite and topaz gems. The bottom was paper-thin layers of silk stacked to create a massive skirt that would trail several feet behind her.

Though Ros was dressed to remind everyone she was of the high Water house, Elsabet downplayed her royal ties. Her dress was a strange color, somewhere between gray and brown depending on how the light hit it. It was floor-length chiffon with a deep cut neckline decorated with stunning lace designs. The sleeves fell back into a sheer cape that flowed the full length of the gown. She was elegant and graceful as always, a true beauty, and even in a gown meant to blend in, Elsa stood out.

Ros moved a stray hair away from her sister's face as she forced a smile. "Time to go."

Elsa nodded. "I'll support you, whomever you choose. I know Mother and Father have their preferences, but contrary to popular belief, I just want you to be happy. So, pick someone who isn't a complete arse."

"Such words of wisdom," Ros teased.

"I'm serious," Elsa said, pushing against Ros's bare shoulder.

Ros turned away from her sister, not wanting to show how much her words meant. As she glanced out the window one last time, she spotted a strange sight moving up the lane. After all the extravagance of those before it, the brilliant exhibitions of elemental mastery, the small carriage moving toward the castle pulled by unadorned horses seemed unusual in its simplicity.

They were beautiful beasts, certainly, but surprisingly plain in comparison with the sights that had come before. There were six of them: a spotless white, a midnight black, a blood bay and a dapple gray, a piebald, and a palomino.

"Who is that?" Elsa breathed, her voice feather-soft.

"I don't know," Ros said. "Maybe they're not here for the Match."

"Of course they are," Elsa said, as if there was no other explanation.

"They could just be coming for the festivities. A noble family wouldn't send their son in a carriage like that, without a display of power."

Elsa inhaled sharply. "Maybe it's Alaric."

Ros's eyes widened at her sister's words. She turned back to the carriage, praying to anyone listening that it would not be Alaric. "I hope not."

"It would be sweet if he came to confess his love."

"It would be a disaster," Ros said. "There's no way Father could let it slide in front of the other guests. He'd have to let him compete..."

"And he doesn't have magic," Elsa said, finishing the thought. "He'd die."

But as they watched the horses draw closer, Ros *knew* it wasn't Alaric. She wasn't sure how she knew or what made her so certain, but she had no doubt that whoever was in the carriage was no magicless man from the village; no, the man in that carriage was dangerous.

And he was there for her.

Ros listened to the applause as her sister descended the grand staircase. She was certain there were plenty of suitors there who would prefer Elsa as the prize for the Great Match this year, but at seventeen, her sister still had three years before her chance.

Of course, as princess of the realm, Elsa would be the intended match of that year. *The prize.* That's simply the way things worked. The highest ranking of the upper class for any year became the object of affection the year they turned twenty. They would observe the competition and choose a victor. Those who weren't chosen during the match were then left to court and make matches as they saw fit. Ros often wondered if the matches after the Great Match were better for it. There was no competition, and though there was always pressure to marry as well as possible, surely some of those matches were made for love.

As the herald read her extravagant list of titles and accolades to the assembly, she prepared to step out from where she stood. She'd practiced several times, not wanting to risk embarrassing herself in front of more than a hundred nobles gathered for the feast tonight. Now, she took a breath to steady herself and nodded for the servant to open the door.

Ros stepped forward onto the balcony overlooking the room just as the herald said, "Heir-apparent and this year's Great Match, Princess Rosalinde Adara Managold."

She looked down onto the room, smiling as best as she could and hoping her anxiety was hidden beneath her veneer of happiness. Beaming faces met hers as the room reverberated with applause. She wondered if any of them felt those smiles on the inside or simply wore them as they were required, an accessory to their fancy attire.

As she moved toward the stairs, Ros tried to wipe the thought from her mind. Kingdoms ran on politics, on cleverness and ambition and pragmatism, not on *feelings*. Her mother had grounded her in those facts through the years, warning her to keep her head on and her heart guarded. For the most part, Ros had listened. She'd had a few dalliances over the years, but none had ever captured her heart. How could they, when she always knew her marriage would end up decided like this?

She was nearly at the bottom of the stairs. Her heart hammered wildly as her gaze flitted around the room, taking in the faces staring up at her. Most she knew, but there were a handful she didn't recognize. She heard the herald calling above her now, shifting the room's attention to the balcony as her mother and father stepped out. She was grateful the assembly's eyes were off her, giving her a slight reprieve from their notice. The coming week would put her at the center of everyone's attention as her every decision was analyzed. This single moment of peace was a haven in a storm.

Just before she reached the last step, Ros's foot caught on her dress and she lost her balance. She felt herself falling, tumbling through the air as if in slow motion. Her imagination ran rampant with flashes of people pointing and peals of laughter, the nobles whispering about what a disgrace she was and how *anyone* would be a better choice, not only for the Great Match, but also to take the throne after her father.

Strong arms grasped her before she could hit the

ground, steadying her against a firm, wide chest. Ros's hands had instinctively raised to break her fall, but instead pressed against the man, feeling his warmth seeping through his black tunic. She stared up into a face she didn't recognize. The man's black hair was shorn close to his head, his sharp jaw shadowed in stubble that stood out against olive skin. His eyes were dark and cavernous; for a moment, Ros felt herself getting lost in them.

It was his lips that drew most of her attention. They were just the right amount of full, and she had a sudden inclination to touch them to see if they were as soft as they looked. Then they twitched up in a smirk that set Ros's insides ablaze. She was certain he was laughing at her on the inside, though he dare not do so openly. Though he had been gentleman enough to help her from falling, he hadn't been kind enough to keep himself from delighting in her embarrassment.

Ros pulled herself from his arms, straightening her dress. She stretched to her full height and tilted her chin up, throwing in as much confidence and defiance as she could muster. She looked the man in those dangerously deep eyes and said, "Thank you, kind sir, for your swift response. I fear I would have been injured without your intervention."

His lips curled a bit more at her words, but he dipped into a bow of epic proportions. When he stood, his voice rumbled, "It was my honor, Your Royal Highness. Always a pleasure to serve the crown."

She wasn't sure if his words were truth or jest, though she suspected the latter. Though he held to all the formalities of polite conversation with someone of her station, she still felt there was something strangely casual in the way he regarded her. It made her uncomfortable, as she wasn't sure how to respond to the man, but at the same time, she was grateful that not every person here was swayed by her position.

Ros glanced around to see who might be watching them. If this man was a suitor, she couldn't be seen spending an inordinate amount of time speaking with him during the beginning stage of the match. She also wanted to ensure that her clumsiness hadn't overshadowed the rest of the evening. Most people still seemed concentrated on her parents as they descended the stairs. When she turned back to say more to the man, he was gone.

"I don't think anyone noticed."

Ros jumped at the whispered words beside her. She turned toward Larkin, happy to see her best friend. She looked ravishing in a deep cut red gown that would have looked indecent on anyone else, but she somehow pulled it off. Larkin's braids were swept up in an elaborate design that drew attention to her sharp cheekbones and long, slender neck. She was an unmitigated beauty. Her umber skin was flawless, her eyes the color of warm caramel. She needed nothing to make her skin shine or her eyes dance—they did that all on their own.

"Did you see where that man went?"

"You mean that fine specimen who caught your clumsy royal self?"

Ros smiled. Of course Larkin would point out how handsome the man was. She had no issue expressing her attraction to anyone. Absolutely *anyone*. Larkin was open to loving whomever she connected with and often spent her time in the company of a wide variety of people, both in the bedroom and out. It was one of the things Ros most admired about her. She appreciated outward beauty, but ultimately it was the person's heart that drew Larkin to them.

"He wasn't exactly pleasant," Ros said, dismissing Larkin's clearly good taste in the looks department.

Larkin shrugged. "That hasn't always stopped you in the past."

"And look how successful those relationships were," Ros said. "Besides, it's not like it matters anyway. Not tonight."

Larkin put her hand around her friend's waist and steered her toward a table laden with goblets. "Let's not discuss the match. Instead, let's drink our weight in wine and refuse to worry about the coming week. I'm very good at pretending bad things don't exist."

"That sounds perfect," Ros said, grateful for the distraction. "Let's find a place to spy on everyone so I can get your opinion before—"

"Rosalinde," the queen's voice cut through the crowd.

Ros sighed and muttered, "Our escape was too good to be true."

She grabbed Larkin's elbow to make sure her friend didn't try to slip off, then turned to face her mother. The queen was smiling, the details of her face unreadable to the casual observer, but Ros knew every aspect, every facet of her mother's many masks, and she knew this smile was hiding something.

"Good evening, Mother," Rosalinde said, trying to put her anxiety under her own false smile.

Queen Sariyah looked from Rosalinde to Larkin and back. "Are you well, darling?"

"Yes, of course," Ros replied.

"It's just, I saw your tumble…"

Ros grimaced. She had hoped her parents were too consumed with their own entrance to notice her flub. "Just the dress and my clumsiness, I'm afraid."

"Good thing that gentleman stepped in. Right, Your Majesty?" Larkin said.

Sariyah's smile tightened at the edges, just enough for Ros to notice. "That was fortunate. Who was the gentleman? I wasn't able to see his face."

"That's too bad," Larkin said. "It's a hell of a face."

Ros elbowed her as she said, "I'm not certain. I didn't recognize him and he was gone before I had the chance to catch his name."

"If you see him again, send him to me," Sariyah said. "The crown owes him its gratitude."

"Of course," Ros replied, dipping her head.

Larkin curtsied as the queen turned from them. Before Sariyah took a step, she turned back and said, "Larkin, dear, make sure you come to visit the next time you stay with Rosalinde. We were sorely disappointed this morning that you didn't join us before darting off to do gods know what."

"This morning?" Larkin asked, before realizing what she was saying. She quickly added, "Oh right, this morning. Yes, I had to go... help my brother. He's competing in the Great Match this week, as I'm sure you're aware."

"Yes, I did hear that. I saw him earlier, though I haven't had the pleasure of speaking with him yet. I must say, I don't remember him looking so handsome."

Ros laughed, unable to help herself. "Zandor? Handsome? I mean, granted, the last time I saw him was nearly two years ago, but he has always been a scrawny thing with his head buried in a book."

"He couldn't have been that small. Didn't you compete in the games against him a few times?" Sariyah asked.

"Jousting," Ros said, remembering her sister's words from lunch about the day she allegedly won his affections. "He was terrible. Zandor could barely hold the lance."

"He's filled out since then," Larkin said with a shrug.

Sariyah tutted. "Don't dismiss him yet. He's grown into quite the looker and may be exactly what you're looking for. And I, for one, am looking forward to seeing his performance at tomorrow's opening ceremony. It would be nice to have another from Earth house around the castle."

Queen Sariyah's eyes flitted to Rosalinde's for the briefest of moments, as if reminding her of their conversation regarding her preference for Rosalinde's future husband. She departed without another word, leaving the girls staring at her flawless open-backed gown as a single string of diamonds caused light to dance between the queen's shoulder blades.

"I love your mother," Larkin said, "but she terrifies me."

"She has that effect."

"And what was that about me being here this morning?"

Ros sighed as she turned back to the table full of wine. She grabbed two goblets and handed one to Larkin as she drank deeply from her own. "Elsa was being Elsa and told my parents that I'd had a guest last night."

"And I was your cover?"

"Of course. You were brilliant by the way."

"Maybe next time you can warn me before I lie to the Queen of Talabrih?"

"There won't be a next time." Ros took another drink of wine and whispered into her cup, "I was saying goodbye to a friend."

Three

S he finished her wine in one swift gulp and leaned her cup forward for a servant to refill. Ros glanced about the room, taking in the glittering jewels draped about the women, the stylish cuts of their dresses, the intricate hairstyles. Many were on the arm of a man in power, suited in finery as elaborate as their wives.

Among them were several women who held their own power, exuding confidence and strength without the need for a man at their side. It had always bothered Ros that there were far less women who held power in the houses. She knew them to be as capable, and often-times more formidable than their male counterparts, and vowed to have many strong women providing her counsel when she took the throne. As the future ruler of the kingdom, Ros wanted to be one of those strong, powerful women, and for years had promised herself she wouldn't be distracted by a man at her side.

Larkin tugged on her arm, pulling her back to the present. She whispered, "You have company."

Larkin slipped away into the crowd as Rosalinde turned to see two men approaching. She knew them both, to her great displeasure. They were cousins from Fire house, Florian and Dryden, though Ros could never remember which was which. One wielded lightning, a product of two fire parents. The other had a mother from the Air house and was firmly between the two with his gift of thunderstorms.

"Your Highness," one of the cousins said. Both bowed their heads in stiff greeting, presenting forced smiles when they met her eyes.

Rosalinde nodded her head ever so slightly in acknowledgement. This was one of the things she hated most about these events. They could be great fun once the formalities were past, but first you had to navigate an ocean of politics and rigid etiquette. Like giving just the right amount of recognition to two nobles you didn't particularly care for.

"You look lovely tonight, Rosalinde," one of them said.

The other smacked his arm and hissed. "Cousin, too familiar. What are you thinking?"

"Calm your fire, Dryden," said the one who must be Florian. He reached past Ros, the velvety sleeve of his doublet kissing her upper arm, and plucked a goblet from the table. "Her Royal Highness surely gets tired of all the posturing when she's simply trying to have a drink."

Florian tipped his cup to clink against hers and drank deeply. Rosalinde's smile turned genuine at the exchange. Previous conversations with the Fire cousins had always been tedious and built on ceremony, or framed with their gallant tales of how they rescued a maiden from a vile beast with naught but their bare hands. Or something like that. Ros often lost the plot during their excessive talking.

But since she saw them at last year's feast, perhaps Florian had changed. She was certainly willing to entertain the thought, and maybe a small glimmer of hope, that he'd grown out of his boisterous, juvenile manner and into a man she didn't hate spending time with. Ros took another sip of wine, reviving the warmth in her cheeks. She said, "I do grow tired of it, yes. And I am perfectly fine with you calling me Rosalinde if I may also call you Florian, rather than your tediously long title."

Florian laughed and swept his fingers through his thick blond hair. Ros was suddenly struck by how handsome the fire mage was. She'd never considered it before, but now she couldn't help but take notice. She supposed that was what happened when one left their awkward teenage years.

As she noticed him now, she wondered when he'd grown so tall, when his arms and shoulders had filled out. He looked well-built, firm, lithe. His skin was deeply tanned, like most of the Fire house, who all seemed to have an affinity for the outdoors. His eyes were made of afternoon sun shining through autumn leaves, golden and glowing.

"It is a ridiculous title, to be sure. Nothing compared to yours, dear Princess, but still. *Florian le Fevre of the House of Fire, firstborn of Lord Gilthroy and Lady Dusswana of Air, wielder of thunderstorms, heir to the blah blah blah*," he said in a mock formal tone.

Ros couldn't help but notice he left out his place in line for the Fire house. But she knew it, of course, and Florian *knew* that she knew. She pursed her lips as that tiny spark of hope that he'd changed turned to dust in her mouth. Perhaps Florian had spoken out of habit, or perhaps he simply couldn't help who he was. Either way, he had reminded her that he was the highest match she could make in his house, though more subtle in the attempt than in years past. She cast a glance to Dryden, noting the new clench of his jaw. So, she wasn't the only one who noticed Florian's reminder.

"Yes, well," Ros said, unsure what else there was to say.

"Are you excited for the Match?" Dryden asked, steering the conversation into neutral territory.

"Of course," Ros said, forcing a bright smile. "Do you have something special planned for tomorrow?"

She tried to listen as Dryden spoke, but found herself distracted from his words while she raked her eyes over him. He was shorter than his cousin, though not by much, and a bit stocky. His blond hair curled over his ears in a boyish way that Rosalinde found endearing. Dryden's nose was crooked, like it had been broken and he hadn't let a Healer tend to it. He was handsome, like Florian, but in a way that was more natural, less polished.

Ros suddenly realized that he had stopped talking and was staring at her as if he was waiting for an answer to a question she hadn't heard. Before she could make a complete fool of herself, Larkin appeared at her side and said, "Rosalinde, dear, I hate to pull you away from such stimulating conversation, but you promised my brother a visit before dinner. Shall we go find him?"

Ros gave the Fire mages an apologetic look and said, "I'm sorry, gentlefellows, but I must keep my promises. If you'll excuse me?"

"Of course," Florian said, a slight crease formed between his brows but disappeared almost immediately. "You'll save me a dance tonight, won't you?"

Rosalinde nodded as Larkin pulled her into the crowd. They were already three steps away before Dryden called out, "Me as well, Your Highness."

Once the girls were out of earshot, Larkin said, "Good grief, that was painful to watch, even from a safe distance."

"That's what I have to look forward to. One of those men is destined to be my husband," Ros said. She made to take another sip of wine, but Larkin grabbed it from her hand.

"I changed my mind about the heavy drinking

tonight. You'll need your wits to avoid getting stuck with the likes of them."

"I'll need the wine to tolerate my time with them. They're all like that, Lark. I'm doomed."

"How fatalistic."

Ros recognized the deep voice. She turned to see the black-clad stranger leaning against the wall, arms folded across his broad chest.

"You," she said, eyes narrowed.

The man's smirk came easily to his face again. He nodded slightly and said, "Me."

"You ran off before..." Ros started. Before what? Before she could hate him more, or thank him again, or wipe that stupid smirk from his handsome face? She pressed a hand to her forehead, realizing she'd had too much wine in too short a time.

"Good evening, sir," Larkin stepped in, curtsying to the man. "Thank you again for helping Princess Rosalinde. As you can surely see, she isn't feeling well tonight."

"Wine can do that," he said. "You should get the girl some bread."

The girl? How dare...

Rosalinde's eyes darted up to him, her mouth falling open for what would surely be a scathing rebuke, but Larkin cut her off before she could say anything. "The queen would also like to give her thanks and has requested you seek her out."

The man's eyebrows lifted, and Ros was delighted

that the queen's request had taken away that infuriating smirk. But as she watched him, she also realized that this man did not try to hide his surprise, or his amusement, from anyone. He wore his expressions with ease. It was a confidence like her mother's, but rather than being built on holding emotions close to hand, his confidence seemed to come from giving everything away.

"Who are you?" Rosalinde asked, giving into the drink and letting the wine loosen her tongue.

An expression crossed the man's face that Rosalinde couldn't quite place. But then his smirk returned and he was giving his full title as all house nobles did: "Cassian Scalise of the House of Night, the child of Ombretta of Shadows, wielder of Darkness, heir to nothing.

HOUSE OF NIGHT. Wielder of Darkness.

Rosalinde couldn't get Cassian's words out of her mind. Though the call to dinner had spared her from any further conversation with him, she couldn't help but wonder what else the son of shadows might have said. And the big question on her mind, the one all other questions led back to: *Why was he here?*

She let her eyes drift down the table, toward the end where Cassian was sitting. She'd dared a glance at him twice already, and both times he'd caught her before she was able to have a proper look. When he'd returned her look the second time with a smirk and tipped his goblet in her direction, she'd turned her eyes away as quickly as she could, feeling heat creep up her neck and onto her cheeks. Though she wanted to believe it was still from the wine, she'd quickly lost all feelings of heady recklessness the moment she found out who the stranger was.

Though the other mages seated near him likely had no idea who he was either, nor what house he hailed from, there was still a distinct distance between his seat and those on either side. There was something about him that left the inescapable desire to flee, and Ros found that even a glance from him sent her heart galloping away, as if it would burst from her body if given the chance.

Her father stood from his seat beside her, interrupting her thoughts. The room fell to silence, all eyes turning to the King of Talabrih as he began his speech.

"Good and noble people, Elementalists and mages of renown, it is my honor to host you this night in our yearly celebration of our great houses. The crown welcomes my kin from House Water," he said. A fine mist fell on the crowd, gentle and refreshing in the heat of the great hall.

"We are pleased to host the great Fire Lords," he said, raising his goblet to the cheers from their side of the table. The candelabras throughout the room seemed to glow a bit brighter with their raised voices.

King Tancred continued, "We welcome our guests from my dearest wife's dynasty, the noble House of Earth." They pounded fists on the table in unison, sending an echo through the room. Each pound of their fists sent a cascade of trees and flowers in extravagant colors blooming around the room, from centerpieces where there previously had been no blossoms to trees and branches sprouting from the walls. Though it was lovely, Ros couldn't help wondering how much time it would take the Water house staff to clean up and make repairs after their display.

"And finally, the esteemed House of Air," Tancred said, taking a drink in their honor as a cool, sweet-scented breeze moved through the room. "I am delighted to see so many familiar faces, to renew the peace between our houses that we've enjoyed these long years, and to share our abundance of mutual respect with those faces that are new."

Ros shot a glance down the table toward Cassian. He drank a toast along with the others, not seeming to mind that his house wasn't received in the king's speech. But how would her father even know to include him? Darkness wasn't *really* an element, just an outlying combination of... something. No one knew for sure what elements made Night house, so they couldn't classify him with any of the others, which is how they came to have their own house despite being few in number.

"As you all know, this is an especially exciting time for myself and your queen. This is the year our lovely daughter finds her husband in the Great Match. We look forward to the competition, and ultimately, to joining the throne to one of your fine houses."

He raised his goblet again, and Ros listened to the

excited chatter return as guests raised their cups and began the feast in earnest. Servants carried platters laden with breads and cheeses, fruits, vegetables, and nuts grown in the queen's private garden, an assortment of meats in various states of preparation.

Ros's stomach grumbled at the sight of it all. She'd missed breakfast while indisposed with Alaric, had felt ill from anxiety at lunch, leaving wine as the only thing she'd consumed that day. She took two medallions of wild boar dripping fig sauce, a heaping of creamy sunchokes, several vegetable slices her mother had grown, and a fluffy, heavily buttered roll.

While Ros lost herself in her plate, the room filled with hearty laughter and raucous stories, tales of feats and failures, epic stories of love and heartbreak, and finally, inevitably, the talk fell to discussing the Great Match. Although Rosalinde tried not to listen to the chatter, she couldn't help but catch words here and there as the entire room discussed her fate as if she weren't even there.

After dinner and dessert, when all had eaten their fill and more, one of the participants in the Great Match worked up the courage to leave his seat and present himself before Rosalinde and the royal family. It was a tradition observed every year, no matter who they were competing for, that each contestant would present themselves for approval in front of the royal family. But this time Rosalinde found the practice suffocating, rather than building excitement as it had before.

The first this year was a fire mage of a lower house. *Nariq,* he had said. *A Combustion mage.*

Rosalinde noted his curls of red hair, his thin-lipped smile. He had a kind face, and if she'd seen him elsewhere she might have assumed him shy. But he was the first to make his way to the front tonight, his confidence belying his innocent appearance.

Others followed, twenty-four in total, from Air and Water, Earth and Fire. Nariq the Combustion mage was one of five competitors she'd never met. The others were Phineer, a Wavemaker, Galagorn, a Botanical mage like her mother, Quisto, a Firedancer, and finally, Graeme, the dark-haired Air mage she'd seen fly in on the wind phoenix. There were others she didn't know well, but she had met them at least once or twice through the years.

The Fire cousins made their way to her father's side, Florian giving her a devilish wink as he stated his title. Larkin's brother, Lyzandor, presented himself, unable to make eye contact with Rosalinde the entire time. A healer who'd been training with her father—Teague— gave her a weak smile as he presented himself. He was a kind man, and an exceptional Healer, according to her father, but he was there to please the king, not for any affection he had for her.

As Orion Bain made his way forward, his gaze never straying near her, Ros clenched her fists tight and willed herself not to stand up and scream. He and Ros had gone from close friends to mortal enemies after what he'd done last time he had visited. Though her parents knew they were no longer close, she hadn't expressly told them what had happened. Ros had incorrectly thought he would have enough decency to stay away on his own, but now that he was here, she would need to address the scoundrel and the memories she'd been doing her best to forget.

Ros sighed. Even without Orion's presence dredging up painful reminders of what had happened, the whole procession was a drawn-out tradition she could do without. In an attempt to honor the royal family, the competitors completely dismissed their future partner. It was nothing more than a power showing, a chance for the nobles to get a look at the competition. Rosalinde found the whole affair tedious and misogynistic.

Fortunately, there weren't as many competitors as Rosalinde had expected. The number changed each year, depending on how many twenty-year-old Elementalists there were at the time. Two dozen seemed plenty enough as it was, and she was grateful there were fewer than previous years. She couldn't imagine the years during baby booms, where there would be more than a hundred mages fighting for one prize. This amount seemed ideal. Less names to remember, less pretense, less forced interactions throughout the week. Less to turn away when she chose her husband.

Her father stood, preparing to thank the participants and their houses, but a chair scraped against the floor in the silence her father had created, drawing all eyes to the heir of nothing, Cassian Scalise. He stood from his chair in a way that could only be described as lazily. Each step he took seemed to Ros to shake the room, though in truth his feet were silent as sin.

Cassian reached the head of the table where the royal family sat, his eyes on Rosalinde the entire time. Though the other houses had made their polite bows, giving nothing more than what was required, Cassian made a show of bowing so deep, his forehead nearly kissed the floor. It was a gesture that sent the other houses into a whispered frenzy and left Cassian's now-familiar smirk in place as he regained his stature.

"Your Majesties," he said. His eyes slid to the queen and he added, "It is a pleasure to see that the extravagant descriptions of your beauty are true."

Sariyah dipped her head toward him and said, "Good sir, I am at a disadvantage as we have yet to make an acquaintance."

"A misfortune indeed," Cassian said. "My name is Cassian Scalise. I believe you've met my mother."

"Oh, lovely," the queen said with a polite smile. "Pray tell, what is your good mother's name?"

"Ombretta of Shadows."

A cough erupted from the queen. At the same time, the assembly in the great hall made a collective gasp at the name. The last time anyone had seen Ombretta, she had been in this very room, speaking with the same two people her son now greeted.

The queen regained her composure as swiftly as she had lost it. "Yes, of course. How fares she?"

"She is well and sends her regards, Your Grace."

Despite Sariyah's calm exterior, the king was visibly shaken. His voice was thin as he asked, "And do you come tonight in her honor, to carry her words and gift us the presence of the House of Night? Or are you here on other business?"

"It is my deep pleasure to represent the House of Night at this feast," Cassian said.

Ros studied his face as he spoke, seeing a genuine delight playing across his dark features. Whatever his motives, he was being truthful in that he was enjoying himself. The shock of the Elementalists around him only bolstered his confidence.

Cassian's eyes met hers and he said, "But I do have other business, Your Highness."

It took Ros a moment to realize he had addressed *her*, not her father. In all her years at feast, even tonight when men came forward to claim a right to her hand, none had addressed her specifically. Not only had he spoken to her, but he waited for her permission to speak.

She took a steadying breath and asked, "And what business is that, Cassian Scalise of Night house?"

"To participate in the Great Match, my lady. To offer my hand in friendship, in honor, and in trust."

"And how is that different from the other men here tonight, good sir?"

"Because I do not regard you as a prize to woo or win with flattery or displays of power. You are a woman; I am a man. I am here to see if our hearts are compatible."

Ros took a steadying breath, but her words were still barely more than a whisper when she asked, "And if they are?"

"Then I am yours, Princess. Mind, body, and soul."

Sixteen heartbeats passed before the ringing in Rosalinde's ears stopped and she was certain of what she had heard. The room sat in stunned silence, waiting for her response, though she had none to give.

After a moment, King Tancred cleared his throat and said, "Well then, best of luck to the Night house mage, as he joins Water, Earth, Air, and Fire in the Great Match."

The king raised his glass in toast, and the rest of the assembly rushed to join him. Cassian held Rosalinde's eyes for a few seconds longer, pinning her to her seat. With a final flash of his infuriating smirk, he returned to his place at the end of the table.

Four

Princess Rosalinde was eternally grateful for her sister's arm as they walked to the courtyard. After Cassian's words at dinner, her mind was spinning so fast that walking on her own seemed like too much for her.

"That was one of the more interesting Great Match dinners I've seen," Elsabet said as they walked. "Some of the older nobles nearly lost their minds when the Night mage revealed himself."

"What do you think he wants?" Ros whispered.

"Besides your—how did he say it?—*mind, body, and soul*?" she said, capturing Cassian's inflection perfectly.

Ros swatted at Elsa's hand. "Be serious."

Elsa sighed. "I don't know yet. I don't trust him, obviously, but I'm not sure what he's after. Just be careful around him, okay?"

"Of course."

The herald announced the sisters as they walked out of the castle arm-in-arm. The simple stone courtyard had been transformed, as was tradition, into an extravagantly decorated outdoor ballroom. Massive fronds arched overhead, dripping with exotic flowers the color of Water house blue. The stones of the courtyard were smoothed out, without even the slightest chip or crack anywhere to be seen. Though the stones would return to normal by the morning, Ros had always found the transformation fascinating.

She didn't have time to observe all the beauty before invitations to dance began pouring in. Because she only had a week to make a decision on who would be her husband, she was expected to use every moment to form her opinion; turning down a dance, and a chance to get to know someone better, was frowned upon. Ros might as well prepare to spend the next couple hours twirling about, even if she'd rather be anywhere else.

After nearly an hour of nonstop dancing, being passed from one competitor to the next, Ros found herself facing Orion Bain. With an outstretched hand and an exaggerated smile, he begged a dance from her. Every fiber of her being cringed at the thought of his hands on her body. No matter how bad it would look, she couldn't bring herself to take his hand.

"Apologies, my lord, but I require a moment before I take the next dance."

Ros turned to step away, but the Fire mage's hand

caught her elbow. "One more dance, Princess, and then I'll let you rest."

She tugged her arm, but he held firm. "I really must insist—"

"Come on, Ros," he said through clenched teeth. "Don't be such a child."

"Stand down, Bain," Dryden said as he stepped up to Rosalinde's side.

Orion sneered. "You think you can make me? You may have the le Fevre name, but I'm the one with the power."

Dryden stepped closer to Orion and said, "Let go of her. Now."

"Or what?"

A shadow appeared over Orion's shoulder, and suddenly Cassian was there. He whispered, "Or you get to find out if the stories about the Night house are true."

Orion released her arm, but didn't back down from the men. "I'm not afraid of you. Either of you."

Cassian's voice was feather-soft as he said, "You should be."

Ros felt a chill run down her back at his words. Whether they truly affected Orion, she couldn't say, but he grumbled something incoherent and shouldered his way past Dryden as he stormed away.

"I had that handled," Dryden said, scowling at Cassian.

The Night mage dipped his head. "I have no doubt, Fire-cousin. You were handling things swimmingly. I was simply here for support, and to try to keep your thunderstorm in check."

Dryden bristled slightly, seeming unsure what to make of Cassian's words. Before he could settle on being angry, Ros wrapped her arm through his and said, "Thank you for intervening. Would you be so kind as to escort me to a seat?"

"Of course," Dryden said, a smile breaking out across his face.

He walked her to a chair at the side of the room. "Would you like me to stay with you?"

Larkin slid into the seat next to Ros and said, "I've got it from here."

Dryden's smile faltered, but Ros said, "I'll be sure to find you for a dance as soon as I'm up again." The words seemed to pacify him, and he left the women to get lost among the dancing crowd.

"What in the world just happened?" Larkin asked. "I saw some commotion from across the room but couldn't get to you."

Ros swallowed, steadying herself. "Orion Bain."

Larkin's jaw clenched at the name. She knew the story—or at least as much as Rosalinde had been willing to tell her. Ros had no doubt that Larkin would've done more damage than Dryden and Cassian combined if she'd been closer only a moment before.

"Do you want to leave?" Larkin asked, her voice quiet.

"No," Ros replied. "I still have quite a bit of dancing to do."

Larkin sighed. "You should dismiss him."

"The match hasn't even started yet."

"But you know you won't choose him. Why keep him around and waste everyone's time?"

"I should let him perform in the opening ceremony."

"He doesn't deserve your courtesy."

The words hung between them. Larkin was right. Even thinking about Orion Bain was more than she wanted to endure, so being around him would be miserable until she sent him away. Still, she felt like she owed it to their parents to keep him for now. His father was Water house born and had grown up alongside her own. When the men had their own children in the same year, it was natural that they would want them to be close, encouraged even. In childhood Ros and Orion were thick as thieves, and their fathers always seemed delighted they got along so well.

When Ros thought about it now, she realized it was part of her father's plan to form ties with Fire house. Choosing a mage from the Fire lords would cement her father's reign, and perhaps her own someday. All the better if the match were a happy one made with two people who had been friends since birth. Ros might've agreed with them, if not for their last encounter.

She gritted her teeth as she remembered the way his hands pawed over her, the way she pushed at him and begged him to stop. But he didn't, wouldn't, listening only to what he wanted from her and not to the girl he'd been friends with for all those years. He'd pushed her against an alley wall while they'd been out playing at being commonfolk. He was strong, too strong; she reached for her magic to defend herself, but as fear coursed through her, she couldn't call it forth.

A passing blacksmith heard her cries and fought Orion off her. The Firestorm mage called down a fury onto the man who'd interrupted him, charring his skin and sending the man to ruin. Not a second passed and regret flooded over Orion. His eyes had looked at the man he'd burned, and then to Ros, the friend he'd betrayed, and without a word, he sprinted away from them. Ros hadn't spoken to him since that night, and he'd avoided Water house on every visit his father had made since. Until now.

Fortunately for the burned man, Rosalinde's father oversaw the greatest healing center in Talabrih's history, and her rescuer was healed. Ros kept him company as he recovered, and they grew close. Closer than she should have let herself get to a magicless man.

But that was over now. She'd said goodbye to Alaric the blacksmith earlier that morning. Now she just had to bide her time until she could say goodbye to Orion as well.

"I'll get rid of him," she finally said. "I just have to do it at the right time."

Larkin shook her head. "If you told someone—"

"No. I'll not have my name dragged around and rumors started because of him."

"You didn't do anything wrong," Larkin said.

Ros nodded. "I know. I...I thought it was my fault, at first. But now I know it was all on him."

"Then why won't you tell your parents what happened?"

"It's been too long," Ros said.

"What he did is inexcusable, no matter when it happened."

"Can't we just let it go and get back to the party?" Ros asked.

"Think about telling someone?"

Ros nodded. "I will."

Larkin grabbed Ros by the hand and pulled her to the drinks table. At least if they were going to be there all night, they could have a little fun.

Ros DRANK and danced with Larkin for the next half hour before duty called her back to the Elementalists she'd been delaying. Her mother had sent Elsabet to intervene before she could have another drink, making it clear that she needed to resume her obligations before the queen herself got involved.

She danced with a slew of mages, including Dryden, but she'd had enough to drink to make the ordeal bearable.

In fact, she barely realized they were telling droll stories and bragging about foolishness as they spun her around the floor. Until Florian le Fevre took her by the hand.

"I was hoping to have the first dance," he said as they twirled together.

"You should have asked sooner."

He smiled. "I asked before dinner."

Ros shook her head. "You only asked that I save you a dance. You didn't specify *which* one."

"I suppose you've got me there, Princess. But I'd hoped to have made a stronger impression on you so that you'd seek me out first."

Ros laughed, unable to stop herself. "Lord le Fevre, you've certainly made an impression. Not the one you wanted to, perhaps..."

Confusion creased Florian's brows. "Are you unhappy with me?"

"Of course not," Ros said. "I am content with you as a competitor in the Great Match. Just as I am content with the others. Well, most of the others."

"Ah, yes. Dryden said there was an incident earlier."

She nodded. "Nothing worth discussing."

"He's from my house. It's my obligation to address it."

"Not to worry, Firstborn of Fire house," Ros said with a smirk. "It's already handled."

"I'd hardly consider a threat from the Night mage as a permanent solution," Florian said.

"It seemed rather effective. But even if it isn't, I can resolve the issue on my own."

"You shouldn't have to."

Ros stopped dancing and took a step back from Florian. "You're right, I shouldn't. But as Orion is here for *my* Match and I can't ignore him, expect to see the situation concluded posthaste. Good night, sir."

She turned and stormed away before Florian could say another word. Ros was angry, and though she couldn't explain exactly *why* his words had affected her so, it felt absolutely dire that she put distance between herself and the Fire mage. She looked over her shoulder to make sure no one was watching her, then she slipped out of the courtyard, past the stone archways of the castle proper, and into her mother's private garden.

The air was tinged with the sweet scent of night-blooming flowers. Ros took a deep breath, pulling the aroma into her lungs and releasing it in a slow breath. The Great Match hadn't even started, and already she was miserable. How could she choose a husband from those men?

As she moved farther into the garden and she was able to put both time and distance between herself and the nobles, Ros finally released some of the tension she'd been carrying all night. She turned the corner to where her favorite spot in the garden was, only to find someone else lounging on the bench under the wide Olacona tree.

"What the—"

"Princess!" the Night mage jolted up, surprised. "What are you doing here?"

"I should ask the same of you. You're in the queen's private gardens, after all."

Cassian smirked as he ran a hand over his head. "Apologies, Your Highness. After the altercation earlier, I thought it best I make myself scarce. I wandered around and found this place, not realizing it was a restricted area, of course."

"Of course," she said, pursing her lips.

Cassian scooted to one side and motioned to the empty seat beside him on the bench. "Would you like to join me?"

"And have someone happen upon us sitting together, alone? That's hardly appropriate."

Cassian laughed. "It's only sitting, Princess." He got a mischievous grin on his face and stood up, taking a step towards her. "Unless you're really here because you're desperate for a dance?"

Ros stared as he stretched out his hands to her. "You can't be serious."

"I can be, I just prefer not to." He took another step towards her.

"If I'm unwilling to sit with you, what could possibly make you think I'd want to dance with you?"

He was close enough now that she could see the unfathomable darkness of his eyes. He whispered, "Because you're still here."

Cassian wrapped one arm around Rosalinde's waist

and took her hand in his other. He led her around the garden to a tune carried on the breeze, accompanied by the chirping insects, lit by the stars. Their gaze was locked as they spun through the night, and Ros felt both lost and found in that moment. When their movements stopped and they stood there pressed together, Cassian's arm pulling her tighter against his chest, Ros felt absolutely breathless.

After a moment, she whispered, "You're a lovely dancer."

"You're quite lovely yourself," Cassian breathed. He reached up and tucked a loose strand of hair behind her ear. "And see? Dancing with me wasn't so bad."

She laughed. "No, it wasn't. In fact, I wouldn't mind doing it again."

"That can be arranged."

Cassian began to sway where they were, their bodies clinging to one another. His eyes seemed to drink her in, and Ros felt herself pouring more into his gaze. She wanted him to see her, to really *see*. She couldn't remember ever wanting anything more.

"Princess?"

She turned toward the voice calling to her, breaking free of Cassian's arms and his gaze. Two figures came into view, adorned in the Water house colors.

"Are you all right, Princess?" one of the guards asked.

"Yes," she said, though in truth her body felt so light she was practically boneless. "I was just..." She glanced back to the spot where Cassian had been, but he was gone. "I just needed a break."

"The king was concerned," the second guard said.

"I will return straightaway. Thank you for finding me."

She returned to the dance with the guards, but her thoughts were still in the garden, in the arms of the Night mage. Ros stayed as long as was required of her before excusing herself. She knew some of the Elementalists would linger, spending the rest of the evening trying to win her father's approval or work to forge alliances before the games truly began. But she wanted no part of it. She'd had her fill of strange things and unexpected alliances for the night. Besides, there were enough things planned for the next few days that she was well and truly happy to be finished for now.

SHE TOSSED ABOUT, unable to sleep. Every time she closed her eyes, she felt as if she was falling into the haunting gaze of the Night Elementalist. With a sigh, she pushed down the covers in frustration, resigning herself to a sleepless night. She just couldn't shake the way he'd held her and the thing he had said at dinner: *I am here to see if our hearts are compatible.* Not "compete in the Match," or "win your hand in marriage," but seek her heart.

The thought sent a shiver through her. In that

moment, she had looked into his deep, dark eyes and seen something there she wasn't sure of. It wasn't lust or desire, for her or power or anything else; no, it was more like... hunger. But that same thing wasn't present when they'd danced only a short time later. Was it all a game to him? If it was, Ros wasn't certain it had anything to do with her heart.

But what could she have done differently? Could she have refused him entry into the Great Match? It had never been done before. No, he would be allowed to compete with the others as tradition dictated, no matter what she believed about him. Though Ros wouldn't admit it to anyone, not even to herself, she was curious to see the mage in action, to see how far he would go.

Part of her truly did want his words to be true, as outlandish as they seemed. And she couldn't deny how easy they had fit together, nor how her body had reacted to the man. Even now, the thought of his chest pressed against her sent a flush through her skin. It was nice to pretend someone was there for her and not just the power that came with her position.

In the end, it wouldn't matter what he said or didn't say; indeed, it was his skill, his strength, and his magical finesse that would decide his future. The Great Match would display the competing Elementalists' skills for the kingdom to judge, and though it was Ros who made the final determination of who would be her winner, the kingdom would have their say, and she would need to decide how much weight to give the people. She could excuse Cassian from the games any time she wished, but her subjects would be furious if she didn't give them the opportunity to see his Night magic at work before she did.

Her thoughts stilled when she heard soft footsteps outside her door. The handle turned. Ros slipped from the bed and ducked behind the massive redwood bedpost, readying her magic at her fingertips but hoping she wouldn't have to use it. Though there were dozens of guests in the castle this night and the week to follow, the royal wing of the castle was off limits. Guards were posted throughout, so it was likely the figure that had slipped through her door would be familiar to her. Still, better ready to defend oneself than trust in the protection of others.

As Ros watched from her hiding spot, the figure moved through the room with familiarity. They walked to the bed and gently lowered themselves onto it. Ros watched a hand reach out across the bed, searching the blankets for her and finding nothing.

"Rosa?"

She stepped out from her hiding spot, extinguishing the magic in her hands. There was only one person who called her that. *Alaric.*

She opened the curtain to let the moonlight shine through the window, bathing the man's features in a soft glow. He smiled then, the expression changing his face into something nearly angelic.

He was beautiful in the same way a stream is

enchanting, the way a sun-kissed mountain could inspire awe. Alaric was like an unexpected snowfall at the turn of the season, surprising and lovely.

But he was non-magical. He didn't feel the pulse of the elements in his fingertips, didn't know the rush of power surging through his bones. He was a local black-smith from an inconsequential family; a quality crafts-man, undoubtedly, but not someone she could marry. Alaric was a good man, but he wasn't the *right* man.

He moved to the window and placed his hands on Rosalinde's waist. He pulled her to him, his mouth finding hers with practiced ease.

Ros had kissed Alaric more times than she could remem-ber, in more ways than she could count. But tonight, his lips felt like those of a stranger. There was an urgency, an elec-tricity buzzing about him that she'd never felt before. It sent currents soaring through her, begging her for more, more.

His hand slipped to the hem of her nightgown. She felt his warm, calloused fingers as they trailed up her thigh. Her breathing was shallow, ragged at his touch. She was desperate to be touched, but was it Alaric she truly wanted?

Alaric's lips moved across her jaw, down her neck, a welcome warmth that waned each time his mouth found a new place to kiss. He moved to her ear, nibbling gently as he whispered her name.

Rosalinde closed her eyes, preparing to relish in the moment that Alaric next kissed her. But instead she saw another man's face in her mind: dark hair, dark eyes—Cassian Scalise.

She pushed away from Alaric, eyes going wide. Her body heaved with excitement, desire, panic.

Alaric's features were sharp, half his face in darkness, half lit by moonlight. But she could see the worry etched at his brow. "Rosa, what's wrong?"

She rubbed a hand at her temple. "Why are you here?"

He chuckled, reached for her. "I thought that was obvious."

Ros took another step back. "You can't be here. Not anymore. We settled that this morning."

"Because of the Great Match?" he asked, a small smile tugging at one corner of his mouth. "It doesn't have to change anything between us. I don't care about that foolish tradition."

"I do," Ros said, surprising herself with the admission. "I'm choosing the man I have to marry. I can't do that during the day and have you here at night."

Alaric pressed his lips into a thin line, his face taking on a serious expression she'd never seen before. "So, don't choose anyone."

She huffed. "Be serious."

"I am," he said. "Don't choose some guy you barely know, someone you don't love."

Ros shook her head. "Then what? The kingdom needs the stability the Great Match brings. It establishes the future rulers of the kingdom and lets the people have some input into who governs them."

"The kingdom will be fine without you giving up your future. You don't have to sacrifice yourself to this simply because those before you didn't have the courage to stand up to these ridiculous games you're forced to play."

"And what happens if I don't participate? I anger the people—"

"It's a celebration day to them and little more," Alaric cut in. "They're not the ones who have to live with your decision."

"They are, though. This decision affects them as much as me."

"They'll adjust."

"And I'm just supposed to what, choose you?"

"Yes, choose me. Is it really so hard to believe I would want that?" he asked, turning away as he ran his hands through his hair.

She sighed and said, "Alaric, we've always known how this would end. We've never pretended it was anything other than what it was. So why now—"

"Because I love you," he rushed, like he'd been holding the words behind a dam that could no longer withstand the weight of them. "I've loved you for a long time, Rosa. I've just been waiting for you to figure out that you loved me, too. But we're out of time."

Ros swallowed, afraid of the words that would come from her if she didn't steady herself. Finally, she said,

"You don't love me. You love rolling around my bed, you love the danger and secrecy, but not me."

Alaric fell to his knees in front of her, pulling her hand to rest against his heart. "Don't tell me how I feel, Rosa. My heart beats for you. Can't you feel it? Don't you know I'd tear the very stars from the sky if you asked it of me? I'd count every grain of sand from here to Vash-nadu. I'd soar on wings of light—"

"Alaric, no," she said, withdrawing her hand.

"Please, Rosa. Tell me you love me. Tell me this meant something to you. Tell me the truth."

She stared down at him, memorizing every line of his face. The dimple on his right cheek, the thin scar through his left brow, the way his top lip dipped to create the most perfect, kissable divot. She ran her hand through his sandy brown hair, and when her periwinkle eyes met his hazel ones, she knew she'd been a stubborn fool. There was no possible way she could've kept herself from loving this man.

But instead, tone flat and hollow to her own ears, she pushed out different words through her numb lips: "You are a wonderful person, but I don't love you. This was just a way to pass the time, and now it's over. You need to leave and never return."

Alaric's face was one of terrible pain, and for a moment she almost lost her resolve. But she didn't. She couldn't. She needed to protect him from this place, this world that was so unfair to those who had no magic. It was cruel to those who sought love, and she wouldn't let

Alaric be ruined by her world. He could still be free to have a fulfilling life if she stepped out of his path.

He rose to his feet, his eyes never leaving hers. "I don't believe you."

"I don't care what you believe," she said. She willed herself to wear her mask just a little longer, not to break in front of him and reveal the pain raging inside.

She turned and faced the window, unable to look at him any longer. She felt him behind her, the tips of his fingers at her shoulder in an almost-touch. Then wordlessly, he left. The door creaked shut and Alaric was gone.

Ros collapsed on the floor the second the door closed. Every part of her wanted to chase after him, consequences be damned. But she knew she couldn't do that, not to him. So she sat on the floor and wept, letting her feelings fill the tears that flooded down her cheeks.

When she could cry no more, she wiped her eyes and stood. She moved across the room to the bed where she'd spent many nights wrapped in Alaric's embrace. As she crawled under the blankets, a movement in the corner of the room caught her eye. She turned toward it, studying the darkness lurking there, but in the end, it was nothing but shadows.

Five

The morning meal was more subdued than the feast from the night before. Many of the high nobles, including the king and queen, had already eaten and left to attend the morning activities. Throughout the day there would be archery, jousting, swordplay, and feats of strength, all unaided by magic. Many of the local magicless folk would participate and claim victories in the games, earning riches and prestige. For the winners, the week of the Great Match provided a year's worth of wages to support their families.

After midday, the first events of the Great Match would begin. Though there would be no actual battles on the first day, the opening ceremony would display the gifts of the mages competing. It was always an exciting time and a favorite among the magicless folk, giving them the opportunity to see powers they'd never seen before, or traditional gifts used in new ways. If they didn't already favor a certain mage before the ceremony began, they would likely choose a frontrunner during, often placing bets on which Elementalist would win the Great Match.

Tradition dictated there would be four judges in addition to Rosalinde at each of the events pertaining to her match, one from each house. The judges were only permitted to vote on the participants from other houses, not from their own, in an attempt to discourage favoritism. Rosalinde considered the judges input a matter of formality. Though they would assign a score so that the participants could be placed in a ranked order, in the end, she could choose to dismiss their votes altogether and choose the lowest scoring competitor if she so wished. It wasn't often done that way, but it had happened in the past when the matches had found love.

She sighed and pushed away thoughts of the Match. It would be here soon enough without her worries. Instead, she tuned in to the conversations around her. There were small clumps of people here and there down the table and throughout the room, and all seemed to be talking about the sudden appearance of the Night house mage.

Now that she was listening, she wished she wasn't. Every scrap of conversation that fell against her ears seemed to whisper, *Cassian, Cassian.* Rosalinde did her best to ignore them, or at least pretend to. She didn't like the way they spoke of him as if he were some sort of mysterious hero, when all she could see was a villain.

The more she thought about it, she couldn't pinpoint any specific wrongs he had done, aside from his obnoxious smirk when she'd fallen, but his very presence felt wrong. He had invaded her home, her one chance to choose her husband, and last night he'd been an uninvited guest inside her head. Not only when Alaric was there, either. She's spent the whole night tossing and turning, running from the wielder of Darkness.

Ros bit into a slice of apple. It was tarter than she expected and her lips puckered in response.

"Princess Rosalinde, please, put those lips away while we're in public. There's plenty of time for that later," a voice purred by her ear.

Rosalinde felt heat crawling up her neck as she turned to see Florian dressed all in black, the Fire house emblem sewn on his left sleeve. She didn't acknowledge his words, instead asking, "Already dressed for the tourney?"

He flashed her a wide grin. "I'm coming off a bit too eager, aren't I?"

She smiled. "Maybe a bit."

Florian motioned to the seat beside her and she nodded that he could sit. He piled a plate with sausage, bacon, and a thick biscuit he coated in butter and honey. Ros watched him dig in, unabashed to be gulping down food in front of the Heir Apparent.

When half his plate was gone, he pulled back as if to take a breath and acknowledge Ros watching him. "Forgive me, Your Highness. I'm absolutely famished. I'm afraid last night I had too much wine and too little food."

"I understand that all too well," she said, her lips curling in a smile. She liked this easy version of Florian, and hoped she would see more of him and less of the posturing noble. Gesturing toward the piles of food along the table, she said, "Please, have your fill."

"The food is good, to be sure, but it's you I can't seem to get enough of."

Ros nearly choked on the drink she was taking. After a second, she said, "Bold words, sir."

"I thought perhaps a bit of boldness would be refreshing."

"Aye," she laughed. "It can be."

"Then let me be bold, Rosalinde." Florian reached forward and took her hand, startling her. Boldness indeed! "I am not here to impress the judges or the other mages. Though I care for your parents' opinions of me, it is your favor I desire. I will have your hand."

Rosalinde's brows rose in surprise. Was this the sort of thing she should expect now after Cassian's forward display last night? She pulled her hand from Florian's and moved for her cup to hide her discomfort. Over the rim she asked, "And how will you impress me, Florian of Fire house?"

He flashed a disarmingly perfect grin and said, "With feats of grandeur, my talents, skills, and prowess in the Match, if it please you."

"And if it doesn't?"

His brows creased for a moment. "It must. That is the way of things."

"I am not interested in tradition for tradition's sake," Ros said. "You may very well impress me, but I'm looking for *more*."

"What more could I offer, Princess? Say the word and I'll give it."

Ros worried her bottom lip for a moment. She wanted honest, real, and telling him outright seemed to take something away from it.

Before she could find a way to answer, a figure materialized beside her. She looked up to find Cassian there, dark eyes smoldering down at her. His voice was urgent, nearly panicked when he asked, "Your Highness, are you in need of rescue?"

"Excuse me?" she asked, looking between him and Florian.

"I saw this wild *bore* spouting his nonsense and thought perhaps you needed a reprieve."

The amusement on Cassian's face was so pure, Ros found herself smiling at the exchange despite the seriousness. Jesting among the nobles was common practice, but generally much more lighthearted. Cassian's direct insult had Florian enraged.

Florian flew to his feet and closed the distance between himself and Cassian. "You dare speak that way to me? Do you know who I am?"

Cassian smirked. "I'm certain every person in the vicinity knows who you are, Fire lordling. And if anyone forgets, you'll be more than happy to remind them with your empty words."

Florian rested his index finger against Cassian's chest. "Don't challenge me, boy, or you won't live to regret it."

"Why? Will you harangue me with your useless talk until I beg for death?" Cassian rested the back of his hand against his forehead and whined, "Oh, woe is me! Fear consumes me, much like flattery and falsehoods have consumed this Fire mage's good sense."

Florian pushed against Cassian and growled. "You've been warned." He started to storm away, but caught himself before he'd made it too far. He turned back to Rosalinde and dipped his head. "Your Highness, I look forward to speaking with you again later, once the rats have been removed from the room."

Cassian laughed as Florian stomped away. He turned to Ros and said, "That was really the best he could come up with?"

"He'd spent so much time preparing his words for me, he likely didn't have time to rehearse a witty response to your banter."

"Good point, my lady. But good banter is so important, I feel a little embarrassed for his lack."

Ros pursed her lips, trying not to smile. "It's a gift, and not everyone can be as blessed as the Night house."

"I do my best. It's always satisfying when my banter is appreciated."

"Indeed. Though I will admit I'm a bit disappointed that I didn't get to finish hearing all the ways I would be wooed by the Fire mage. He seemed to have an extensive list."

Cassian bowed low to her and said, "Forgive my intrusion into your conversation. If you wish it, I will apologize to the halfwit and give my oath never to rescue you again."

Ros laughed. This was a completely different man than the one she'd met the night before. The Cassian from the banquet was mysterious and dark, wearing either a scowl or a smirk. This man who told jokes and laughed so freely was incompatible with the man who had haunted her dreams.

"Not to worry. Things were deteriorating rapidly." She smiled. "I'm always grateful to the kind soul who saves me from whatever disaster I've landed in."

"Ah, but this one isn't entirely your fault. Men make disasters of themselves in the presence of great beauties. You just have the bad fortune of being lovely."

Ros was grateful the Night mage chose that moment to fill his plate rather than look at the burning in her cheeks. After he'd gathered a vast array of food, he bowed again, though not as deeply as before, and said, "Forgive me, Princess, but now I must take my leave."

"You won't join me to break fast?"

"I have much to do before the tournament this afternoon. Best I am on my way."

"Practicing for the event?" she asked. She wasn't sure why she was postponing his departure, but something about his desire to leave made her want him to stay.

"No, nothing like that," he chuckled. "I must care for my horses before I attend to business in town."

"We have grooms to assist with your horses."

"That's kind, thank you, but I prefer to handle them myself. I care for them daily, so it would be easier for them if I'm there. They know me."

"Six horses?" she asked, remembering the simple carriage from the night before. "Each a different color."

He smiled as he bit into the apple in his hand. With a nod of farewell, he left without another word.

AFTER PERUSING the other events happening before the opening ceremony, cheering on her favorite Water house guard in the sword fighting arena, and purchasing several items from local artisans, Rosalinde had made her way to the arena and now stood behind the curtain in the royal booth. She watched the seats fill as nobles and commonfolk filed into the rows side-by-side. There were no specialty seats, no preferential treatment, just open air and the best view for whomever reached the stadium first.

As her eyes wandered the quickly filling seats, she saw Larkin climbing the steps toward her. She wore a plain green dress and tall brown boots, a far cry from the extravagant red gown she had worn the night before. Still, she was lovely in her house colors, and one look at her told you she was anything but common.

"Good day, Princess," Larkin said, giving a small curtsy as she slipped behind the curtain to join Ros after the guards waved her through.

Ros rolled her eyes at the gesture. Larkin knew how much Ros hated the formality of every little aspect of her position, so she regularly did her absolute best to hold up those very traditions that Ros disliked. Like the curtsy. And using her title in place of her name. If anyone else had done it, Ros would be beyond annoyed. But since it was Larkin, she was only halfway to annoyed.

Larkin picked at a plate of hors d'oeuvres as a servant passed them, pulling away some sort of stuffed mushroom and what appeared to be a fig tart. She offered one to Ros, but looked thankful when she waved it away. With a mouthful of mushroom, she asked, "Nervous?"

"More than I should be."

Larkin wiped her hand down her dress, then grabbed Ros's hand and squeezed. "You're going to have to spend years with one of these fools. Nervous is probably in line with where you should be. I'd be more worried if you were excited."

Ros laughed. "You know, one of those *fools* is your brother."

"Oh, I know. He's probably the worst of them all."

"You don't mean that," Ros said. "Zandor is a good fellow."

Larkin nodded. "Aye, he is, but don't tell him I said so."

"Of course not. If he thought you had something

nice to say about him, he'd surely pass out from the absurdity of it all."

"I love my brother. He's smart and kind, generous. And he's got a good head on his shoulders. If you chose him, he would do his best to make you happy. But that doesn't mean he would be a good king."

Rosalinde's eyes widened at her words. "What are you saying?"

Larkin sighed. "You have to pick someone you can live with, someone you can work with through the years to make Talabrih the best it can be. I would be delighted to have you as my family, but there's more at stake here than what would make us happy. You're not just picking a husband this week—you're picking our king."

Ros swallowed. It was something she already knew, but hearing the words spoken by someone else made everything feel more real. This wasn't just a match for a high noble's hand. She had to make a match for her whole kingdom.

"Are there any you would pick, if you were in my position?"

She surveyed the men lining up below them. "I honestly don't know what I would do. But I'm glad I'm *not* you."

"Not helpful."

Larkin smiled. "You'll make the right choice. I believe in you."

"Are you two having a moment?" Elsabet asked as she stepped into the royal box.

Larkin said, "That's basically all we do. I'm surprised you don't already know that, little spy."

Elsa grinned. "You say that like it's an insult."

"What do you need, Els?" Ros asked, trying to stop them from taking their squabble too far.

"I don't *need* anything, sister. I came to support you. But I can leave, if you don't want me here."

Rosalinde's features softened. "Of course I want you here."

Larkin's face registered surprise for a moment before she muttered, "Right. I'm related to a competitor."

"Yeah, too bad," Elsa said, mock sincere. "Guess you'll have to watch from somewhere else. Might I suggest as far from here as possible?"

"You just want to watch me walk away. I don't mind fueling your naughty little fantasies, kiddo," Larkin said. She blew Elsa a kiss as she started to leave.

Elsa rolled her eyes. "In your dreams, Zolto."

Ros smirked, unable to hide her amusement. Elsa had never told Ros her preferences one way or another, and she hadn't shown interest in anyone as far as Ros had noticed. But as she did indeed watch Larkin walk away, it seemed possible that Larkin might've been more accurate than she realized. The tension between the two was palpable, and something about it felt different than their normal bickering. Elsa's skin was flushed, her lips pressed tight, in a rare peek under her mask.

She wished her sister would confide in her more. The idea that they might someday be close was a hope Ros held dear. But she would never force Elsa to confess something she wasn't ready to talk about. Her sister was welcome to love whoever she wanted and Ros would always support her. Hopefully Elsa knew that.

After a few minutes, Elsa's calm exterior was back in place. Ros didn't bother asking her about the encounter, afraid it would cause her to clam up. Instead, she gestured down to the men receiving their instructions and asked, "Do you have a favorite?"

Elsa surveyed them with detached interest. Finally, she said, "I'll have a better idea after they show their skills today. Right now, I'm leaning toward William Delaney."

"Really? Another Water mage?"

Elsa nodded. "He specializes in Hurricanes. It would be a good mix with your Tsunamis if we ever went to war."

"War?" Ros asked. "Good grief, Elsa. Why would you even say that?"

Elsa didn't look up at her sister, but kept her eyes on the men below as she said, "Take it from someone who spends a great deal of time lurking and listening to things she isn't supposed to: we aren't that far from the possibility of war. A misstep here, a misunderstanding there. The Air house is already growing bolder than Father would like. That's why he wants you to marry from Fire. It would establish his allegiance from three houses and make it less likely they would attack."

"You know about that?"

"Of course," Elsa said, rolling her eyes. "And I know

Mother wants to secure a stronghold for Earth house. The problem is that the houses are so loyal to themselves, they have no room in their hearts for the throne. Father needs to disband the houses and make them all pledge loyalty to Talabrih, but he won't."

"Why not?"

"A lot of reasons. Too many to go into right now. But the basics are that it would be hard, he would have to start fights with the house lords in the hopes of stopping an all-out war, but might end up with one anyway. And you know how he is. He'd rather try diplomacy and believe the lies these people spout at him than make a decision that would require bloodshed."

"I had no idea you were so interested in politics."

"I'm not," Elsa said. "I just figure you'll end up with some schmuck of a husband and you'll need my help running the country."

"Except you're only three years from being married off and living with a schmuck of your own."

Elsa shrugged. "I don't plan on getting married."

"No?" Ros asked with a soft chuckle. "How are you going to manage that?"

"We'll see. A lot can happen in three years."

A horn blew. The four house judges made their way to their seats just below the royal box, signaling the start of the Great Match. Ros and Elsa moved to their seats, but Ros could hardly keep herself contained. She found herself leaning forward with nervous excitement. She looked down at the empty pit dug far below the raised seats of the spectators. The arena's seats formed a circle around the area, with excited viewers on all sides. She saw clumps of orange, green, silver, and blue throughout the stadium denoting groups from each house. For the most part, the full stands looked like a beautiful kaleidoscope of color.

In addition to the house members cheering on their participants, there were townsfolk from near and far filling the arena, waving flags of different colors, and cheering for their favorites. From her time out in the local towns and villages during previous festivals, Ros knew the competitors' families often paid people to walk the towns and gather supporters for them by telling wild, heroic stories. Sometimes they even made promises of payment for the person who cheered the loudest.

Though the challenges through the week would be surprises for the contestants, the opening ceremony remained the same each year—it was a chance to display their power. The men would've prepared something spectacular for their individual events, often practicing for months at a time before performing at the Great Match. It was always one of Rosalinde's favorite times, showing a glimpse into the men's creativity as well as their ingenuity.

Queen Sariyah slipped into the royal box and sat down with her daughters. Ros looked for her father to follow, and when he didn't, worry crashed into her gut. She couldn't recall a single time he'd missed the opening of the Great Match.

"Where's Father?" Elsa asked, seemingly feeling the same sense of dread.

"I don't know," the queen said, barely able to be heard among the rumbling of the cheers.

Ros said, "But the Match—"

"I know," Sariyah cut her off. "He disappeared shortly after breakfast. I've sent a squad of guards to find him, but we must keep this quiet in the meantime. Smile, perform, and let no one know something is amiss."

Ros and Elsa both opened their mouths to protest, but the queen held up her hand and mouthed, "Trust me."

There was nothing else to do. Queen Sariyah was a wise woman, and if she said this was the best course of action, the girls believed her.

A herald's voice broke into Rosalinde's thoughts as they called, "Esteemed guests from near and far, it is with great honor that I present your heroes."

The men paraded in a circle through the ring. All wore the same black clothes; the only color was the emblem on their arm denoting their house. As they marched to the clapping and cheers, the chanting of their names, Ros noticed a current of murmuring running under their excitement. Her eyes trailed the voices, trying to pinpoint their source.

Cassian.

He was last in line, and as he passed those cheering for their houses, they saw the emblem missing from his arm. Ros knew that chatter of the Night house mage would've already made it to the townsfolk, but seeing their awe in person was quite another matter.

The men stopped in front of the royal box. Without the king present to give direction, the order of performance should fall to Sariyah. Ros looked at her to say as much, but the expression on her mother's face was one of utter distress. Her features were unguarded and she was clearly unable to take the advice she'd just given her daughters.

Rosalinde leaned to Elsabet and said, "Get her back to the castle." Then she stood and stepped into the sunlight for all the people to see.

If they were surprised to see her, they didn't show it. Instead they cheered louder than they had for the competitors. Ros smiled and waved at her people, letting her nerves calm while they applauded.

When they quieted, she called, "My fine Talabriheans, it is my deepest pleasure to stand before you today, with my future husband. Can someone please tell me which one he is?"

The stands erupted in laughter, in the chanting of their favorite's names, in the cheers of her own name. She smiled and continued, "We will begin the games with Air, followed by Earth, then Fire, and finally, my honored Water house."

Though there were cheers, the murmuring returned. Ros raised her hands to quiet them and said, "Have I forgotten someone?" She laughed when she saw a little boy jumping up and down as he pointed at Cassian. She met the dark mage's eyes as she said, "Ah, yes, our mysterious competitor from Night. As all things must come to an end as darkness falls, so shall we end our opening ceremonies with the wielder of Darkness."

The crowd seemed pleased with her pronouncement, so she added, "Let the Great Match begin!"

Six

The competitors filed away, leaving the first man from Air house, Merritt Mahone. Ros tried to write his name on a card when he was announced so that she might give him a score based on his abilities, but her hands were trembling. She wished she hadn't sent Larkin away. She needed someone, anyone to be with her right now.

But she was alone and she had to be strong. It was what her mother wanted and what her people needed. She may only be a princess right now, but someday she would lead them. She wasn't sure she was ready to do that, but right now she didn't have much choice. So she worked to settle her nerves, knowing that despite it all, she had to be here, in this moment for her people.

Rosalinde placed her hands on her legs and took several deep breaths. She watched Merritt perform, though she found it hard to concentrate on him. His focus was Gales, and he had placed colored paper throughout the arena that he sent flying in beautiful designs through the air above him. It was lovely, but nothing she hadn't seen before. Nothing to distract her from her missing father and a mother who had looked like a lost child.

She gave him an average score as the next mage took his place. Brensen Cavoll was next, a Stormcalmer who'd been particularly helpful to Ros when she was younger. When her Tsunami powers had raged when they were first learning their gifts, Brensen had been brought to Water house to train at her side. His soothing nature was easy to be around, and it had hurt Ros quite a bit to lose him when his family returned to Air house. She hadn't been close to him after he left, but she still held fond memories of him. Unfortunately, Stormcalming required an actual storm to show his abilities, so the crowd wasn't nearly as impressed with Brensen as Ros felt he deserved.

That was the way of these events. The quiet abilities were overlooked in favor of the flashy entertainers. Fortunately, she would be able to make the final decision, no matter what happened in today's power display.

Another wind mage swirled colored paper through the stands. Ros hadn't caught his name, and with his back to her, she wasn't positive who it was. She thought it was the Surrick boy that Larkin had been interested in a few summers back, which essentially ruled him out for that reason alone. The ties between her and Larkin were worth more than that.

Ros sat up a bit straighter when the herald announced Graeme, the one who had flown in on a phoenix of air. She was unsurprised, but still delighted, when he conjured his nearly invisible bird to fly around the stands. He let the phoenix fly up, up, up until he was barely a dot in the sky.

And then he fell.

The crowd gasped, Ros along with them, lost in the seconds that ticked by as Graeme plummeted toward the ground. At the last second, his phoenix swooped up and plucked him from the air, mere inches from death.

The stands erupted in applause, his name echoing through the arena. Graeme flew his bird slowly past the royal box and blew a kiss at Rosalinde, sending the crowd into an uproar. With his death-defying opening display, Graeme had just made himself a frontrunner.

Ros gave him highest marks. Not only had she enjoyed the thrill of his performance, but she had watched him hold the people in the palm of his hand. He went from an unknown participant to their favorite in seconds. A king should be able to sway the people to his side, even if there was a little trickery involved.

It also helped that he was rather handsome. His dark hair was thick and swept back from his face as he sailed through the air. He was clean shaven, with a jawline so sharp it could cut glass. As he made another pass by the royal box, Rosalinde saw his bright blue eyes aglow with excitement, and perhaps a little mischief.

It was easier to pay attention after Graeme's performance. Though she couldn't fight the worries tumbling over one another in the back of her head, she could quiet them for a while and give her attention to the future King of Talabrih, whoever he might be.

The final mage from Air house was Jericho Tevachaly. Ros had known him all her life, had even had a crush on him when they were in their early teens. Jericho's gift was a rare one among the Air house: Spirit Projection. He stood in the center of the arena, while a faint silver version of himself walked through the crowd. It spooked quite a few people at first, until his spirit started dancing. Spirit-Jericho popped up throughout the stadium, even in the royal box beside Ros, determined to make the crowd laugh with his boisterous kicks and lewd thrusts. By the end, he had them eating from the palm of his hand.

Ros liked Jericho and had always found him to be enjoyable company. Of all those competing, she was certain he was the one who would be the most fun. But then she thought about what Larkin had said. A king had to be more. She rated him slightly higher than Merritt, but Graeme still led the pack.

Next came Earth house. Beckett, the Botanical Elementalist, dazzled the crowd with flowering vines that snaked through the stands, over handrails, and trailed down into the arena. They converged in the center to encircle a massive willow tree that sprouted from the arena floor. The willow was far larger than a natural tree, its branches spreading wide across the space until it formed a canopy over the whole assembly, blocking out the slightest hint of sunlight.

Ros wished her mother or Elsa had been there to see him. They would have a better idea of how hard he had worked on his show, and perhaps a better appreciation for his skill. Without their input, she ranked him alongside Jericho.

Two more Botanical mages came next, but even Ros could see they weren't as skilled as Beckett, so scoring them was easy. Ros was surprised there were so many mages with similar styles one after another. With Earth house, the powers were either green or ground; Elementalists from Earth could grow anything if they were on the "green track," or could manipulate the earth itself if they leaned "ground." But within those broad looks at power, there were nuances Ros couldn't begin to understand.

So, maybe the three mages were vastly different, but to Ros's untrained eye, and likely the eyes of the crowd, it simply appeared that there were three similar mages in a row, and the one with the biggest display of power seemed like the best.

A Seismic mage came next, sending the whole arena shaking. After only a few seconds, a small child fell from the stands due to their shaking. Graeme and his air phoenix swooped up and saved the child from injury, and Graeme used the opportunity to sail the little boy around the arena as the crowd chanted his name, before delivering the frightened and exhilarated child back to his parents. The Seismic mage was booed from the arena, his performance ended before it had a chance to really start.

When another Botanical came next, the whole stadium groaned. Earth house's many competitors were fatiguing the crowd, and having the misfortune of going after the Seismic mage did nothing for the man's performance. He rushed through it, appearing more eager to end the show than to demonstrate his power.

He was followed by a Land Builder—a highly sought gift when nobles wanted to build a home in an inhospitable location. The crowd seemed to like him, but then, Ros already knew Rylen Fielder was a bit of a showman. She wasn't surprised he was able to charm the spectators; he had charmed her too, which was why she gave him low marks. Fool her once...

The final contestant from Earth house was Lyzandor Zolto, Larkin's older brother. Ros watched him with interest, both because he was her best friend's brother and because of what Elsa had said about him having feelings for her. She couldn't say whether or not it would've mattered if she'd known about his alleged feelings before now, but there was at least a small part of her that was looking at him a little differently.

She had to admit, her mother was right about him growing into his looks. Zandor had not always been handsome. As kids, he had never seemed to fit right inside his body. He was the shortest of the bunch, always struggling to be accepted by the "big kids" who were usually younger than him. When they hit their teens, the opposite held true; Zandor sprouted up before anyone else, turning into a gangly, skinny mess.

Now though...goodness...his body was just right. She wasn't sure how she'd missed him the evening before, but somehow his changes hadn't registered in the face of everything else going on around her. She was looking now. He was tall and broad-shouldered, his muscles pressing against the standard black uniform and filling it out a bit more than the other men did. He kept his head shaved smooth, though his face sported stubble, as if he hadn't shaved for a few days. He had the same high cheekbones as his sister, the same caramel eyes. But his jaw was squared where hers was rounded, his lips not as plump but definitely biteable.

Rosalinde shook away all thoughts of Zandor's lips. That was a road she could not go down, *would* not go down. Though she and Larkin had never expressly talked about such things, she felt like it was automatically part of the deal when you became best friends. No matter what, she couldn't choose Zandor.

He began his performance. It was like nothing she'd ever seen. Zandor and Larkin were both metal wielders. She'd seen them work before, but not like this. She'd always thought they had to start with metal to create, never realizing they could make the metal as well.

And that's what Zandor did. He drew particles of metal from the ground, specs of minerals flying through the air, creating a miniature light show as they swirled in the sunlight. It was enchanting. Ros found herself leaning forward on the railing, watching the gleam of metal as it sailed through the air above her, spiraling together like a river of particles as fine as dust. It wasn't until the metal stopped moving that she looked down to Zandor and realized what he had done with it.

In the center of the arena was a statue, a perfect replica of Rosalinde. She covered her mouth with her hand, surprised and overwhelmed at the swell of emotion in her chest. She moved out of the royal box and descended the steps. The arena was silent as she moved, as if every person held their breath, waiting to see what she would do.

She had gone about halfway down when Graeme stepped into the air in front of her, holding out his hand for her to join him on the phoenix. She took his hand, accepting his kindness as he conveyed her down to the arena floor. After landing, Graeme withdrew without a word, leaving her face to face with Zandor and his creation.

Ros walked around the statue, taking in each tiny detail. This was not the work of someone who had seen her from a distance; no, this was a creation from someone who knew her intimately, who had studied every facet of her features and found them to be worthy of attention.

Zandor had been quiet as she walked around the statue, but when she completed her circle and stopped in front of him, he asked, "Do you like it?"

Ros felt a bubble of laughter rise out of her throat.

"Like it? Zandor, it's unbelievable. It's magnificent. I love it."

Zandor smiled broadly and said, "I'm glad. It took me a while to get it perfect."

"It's not quite right," she said. "This version is prettier. She is more confident than I could ever be. This is the version of me I wish I could be."

"That's who I always see when I look at you, Rosalinde. It's hard to believe you don't see it, too."

His words caught her off guard. Ros always thought people saw her the same way she did: clumsy, nervous, easily embarrassed. To hear him say that he saw her in such a magnificent way every time he saw her...she had no words.

She stepped toward him and motioned for him to lean down. Ros said, "Thank you," and pressed her lips to his cheek.

The crowd went wild.

She took a step back, still very close to him, and stared up into his eyes. Through all the people chanting his name, the yells and cheers and catcalling, she barely heard Zandor say, "You're welcome, my love."

Rosalinde's breath caught in her throat. Her eyes met his as she tried to puzzle out his words, his true meaning. Had he truly felt this way for so long without her knowing or was this just part of the performance? But no, Zandor wouldn't say such a thing without meaning it. It wasn't who he was.

Before she could respond—but what could she say?

—Graeme was beside her, offering his hand to return her to the booth. She looked over her shoulder as the statue was returned to the earth from whence it came. It filled her with sadness, but also a strange sort of peace.

She gave Zandor the highest score possible. Larkin might not agree with that decision, but in the end, she needed to follow her heart. Perhaps her heart was leading her to Lyzandor Zolto.

WHEN RED-HAIRED NARIQ the Combustion mage made his way into the arena, Ros almost felt sorry for him. His tricks were fun and enjoyable to watch but, as if reading her mood, the crowd wasn't interested.

Though they'd had a break after Zandor's performance, their thoughts were still on the boy from Earth house, the boy who had never been anything more than a *boy* to her. She looked down to the edge of the arena where the competing mages watched after they had performed. Lyzandor Zolto certainly wasn't a boy any longer.

Ros gave Nariq a mediocre score, though in truth she'd spent more time watching Zandor's profile as he watched the show than actually paying attention to Nariq.

When the herald announced the Fire house cousins as one performance, Rosalinde perked up. She'd never seen two competitors join together, even if they were related. Showing individual skill was how you stood out. But Dryden and Florian le Fevre were always together, always playing off one another in every other aspect of their lives, so why should this be a surprise?

They emerged from opposing sides of the stadium moving toward one another. There was a strangeness to their movements, almost as if they were part of some ethereal dance. One would move forward, the other back, hands swaying above them as if they could repel and attract the other.

The crowd seemed confused by their actions. Their voices rose to muttering as they turned against the mages. There was no display of power, no strength to judge or humor to laugh at. To Rosalinde's surprise, she even heard booing.

She crossed her arms over her chest as she began to take on the same attitude as the crowd. If this was the kind of performance they thought would impress her—

Crack!

Thunder clapped around them as lightning repeatedly flashed above the stadium, arcing overhead like a dome of electricity. Ros looked down at the mages standing in the center of the ring, hands joined above their heads. When their touch broke, the thunder stopped its deafening roar and the lightning stopped curling above.

Dryden and Florian moved away from each other, weaving forward and backward, leaning in and away. This time, the crowd watched with more attention, eager for the moment their hands touched. When the thunder and lightning exploded above the stadium, the people erupted in cheers. The lightning danced above in patterns and designs unlike anything Ros had ever seen. The thunder echoed and crashed and boomed in a cacophony of sound, a symphony built from nature's melody.

It was a beautiful performance. The rhythm and wake of their movements was a surprising element that Ros found herself enjoying more and more as they continued. But when it came time to judge, she had a hard time with her score. Yes, it was lovely and a great display of teamwork, but she wondered what would have happened if they had performed as individuals. Without the drama of their joint performance, would it have been flat?

She couldn't marry them both, and didn't want to judge them both as one. Ultimately, she gave them the lowest scores she had thus far simply because it didn't feel right to score them higher when the other Elementalists didn't have the benefit of a partner.

The cousins were followed by a Flamethrower, a Light Conjurer, and a Suppressant. Like those from Fire house who had come before, none were particularly impressive. The Suppressant gave the best performance when he had all of the other Fire mages who wielded flames to throw their power at him, and he caught and extinguished each attack. It was one of the more inter-esting and rare gifts—built from combining a Fire father and Water mother—but displaying it in an arena wasn't an easy task. Still, Ros rated him higher than the others, knowing it would've taken far more creativity to come up with a power display when your gift was actually extinguishing power.

The next mage from Fire house was easily the best performer from their house. Quisto, the Firedancer Ros hadn't previously met, put on a daring show wherein he grasped and flung fire throughout the arena, pulling it close and pushing it away with his will. He somehow made the fire feel alive, and the display gave a strange, intimate feel to the relationship between the Elementalist and his power. It was mesmerizing.

The last Fire house competitor was Orion Bain.

Ros started when she heard the cheers from the crowd. Orion must've impressed them. She couldn't bear to look at him. The nerve it took for him to be here, to compete for her hand after what had happened, was beyond belief.

Finally, Orion left the arena and Rosalinde's own house performed. The Water mages were spectacular, as she expected. Elsa had predicted a strong display from William Delaney's Hurricane powers, and she had been right. He had a mastery over the element that was far superior to many of the strongest mages Ros had ever seen. The Rain mage, Nicolai Bardeaux, was a powerhouse as well.

Phineer Gohn was next. She'd wondered how she'd never met him as he was a Wavemaker, implying he had two Water parents, but then she realized who those parents were: Stefania and Ashis Gohn, the supremely gifted Water mages who traveled through the country to provide fresh water to smaller towns and villages that didn't have adequate access. Phineer had been raised to believe that sacrifice and giving were the greatest things a man could do. Someone with those ideals would make a good king.

He'd chosen several children from the stands and taught them to surf along the waves he made. Though his waves weren't particularly strong or large, Ros suspected he could do more with them if he desired. Phineer simply didn't seem all that interested in showing off. It didn't matter. The crowd loved him anyway. Maybe they could sense that gentle strength as well.

Ros smiled as Phineer finished his display and nodded in her direction. She was proud of her house's performance so far.

The last Elementalist from Water house was a quiet man with whom Ros was only slightly acquainted through her father. Teague Vannoy was a Healer, and she had seen him in the medical center when she'd visited, but her only interaction with him had been the occasional nod of acknowledgement. When he came into the arena, his gentle demeanor remained as calm as always.

Ros was worried, unsure what he could do. She'd seen her father perform miracles, knew there were many mages capable of immense healing magic, but she had no idea how he would show that in the ring.

He held up his hands and began to turn in a circle. Ros watched with rapt attention, but nothing happened.

A scream pierced the air. Another. Three, four, a dozen. Rosalinde's eyes flicked throughout the stadium as people jumped to their feet sobbing, yelling, clapping. She watched them embraced by those around them as they all cried together. She looked back down to the man who continued to spin, eyes closed, face upturned toward the sky.

He was healing them. All of them.

Ros had never seen anything like it. In fact, the very idea was unheard of. Her father was a skilled Elementalist and could only heal two, maybe three at once if their wounds were minor. This man was healing dozens.

There was a collective gasp as Teague hit the ground. Two Water house medics ran to his side. The whole arena watched with bated breath until finally, finally one gave a thumbs up to the crowd. The Elementalist had clearly exhausted himself and depleted his magic. Ros wasn't sure how long it would take to recover from such an act. The sheer power displayed was remarkable.

Top score. No one could top what he'd just done.

As the medics carried Teague from the arena, a man in all black, no markings, entered the ring. A fitting end to the ceremonies, as dusk was beginning to settle. Now was the time of the Night mage. Now was the time to see the gifts of Cassian Scalise.

Seven

⤜∾⤛

Cassian took a moment to roll up his sleeves. Ros found herself smiling at the gesture. He wasn't worried about the crowd or displeasing them; no, if anything, he was delighting in delaying their show. He knew that no matter what he did, the people's attention would be his, simply for who he was.

He leaned his head side to side, stretched his neck, and looked up to the darkening sky. Ros presumed his gift was stronger at night, which was partially why she'd placed him last. She couldn't deny she was just as eager to see his performance as the rest of them, and she wanted to give him the best chance to show what he could do.

Cassian turned to face the royal box and bowed deeply, as usual. He held out his hands as if to ask Rosalinde's permission. When she nodded, he disappeared.

There were shocked gasps as everyone looked around the arena. But Ros knew where he was. She'd heard his boots land behind her.

Without turning, she said, "Grand display, Cassian, truly."

He laughed. "How did you know I was here?"

"You may be able to hide from my eyes, but you aren't so skilled at deceiving my ears."

"Ah, but now I know to be more careful next time, Princess."

They stepped forward together so the crowd could see them side by side. As the spectators cheered, Cassian held out his hand and asked, "May I?"

Ros looked at his outstretched hand, the playful smile on his lips. She felt her heart jittering in her chest, urged on by the thrill of the unknown. "What are you doing, Lord of Night house?"

He grinned. "Honestly, I'm not sure. I haven't tried this with another person before."

"Then we shall have an adventure."

He laughed. "It may fail spectacularly."

"Then I'll just have to rate your dancing instead of your performance."

Cassian stepped behind her so his right hand could hold her right, and he put his left on her waist, whispering, "Put your other hand over mine."

As soon as she did, there was a strange sensation that passed through her body. Time slowed and stretched as they moved—however they moved—through space. It wasn't darkness that surrounded them as she had expected, but the most beautiful, brilliant colors she had ever seen. And Cassian was there beside her through the whole thing, watching her as she watched everything else.

When he released her, they were in the stands next to a little girl with brown pigtails and freckles. The girl dipped into a sloppy curtsy and stuttered, "Milady."

Cassian stepped forward and shook hands with the girl's father. "John, good to see you again."

"And you, Lord Cassian. I can't thank you enough for what you did for my family."

Cassian shook his head. "I did nothing, sir, except make a request of our grand Healer. But it is nice to see Sasha standing on her own."

"Aye, it is," John said, wiping a tear from his eye. He pulled the little girl to him and kissed her on the head. "Thank you, milord. And you as well, milady. We shall never forget what happened here this day."

John grabbed Rosalinde's hand and pressed cracked lips against it. A moment later, Cassian held her again and they moved through the light.

They appeared on the other side of the stadium where a woman grabbed Cassian by the shirt and began kissing his cheeks. She finally stopped and bowed to Ros.

Ros took her arm and said, "Please, tell me what's happened."

"The Lord of Night, milady, he came through the

village this morning. Said he wanted to see the people, those who were sick and injured. Said to make sure to be in the stands today." The woman pointed at the man standing beside her, his wrinkled face tear-streaked. "My husband has been sick for years. Coughing, trouble breathing. He just took his first real, deep breath in a long time."

Ros looked back to Cassian. "You arranged all this?"

In answer, he swooped his arms around her and they disappeared again. They were in the center of the ring now, the crowd clapping for him. Ros looked at him, brows raised, waiting for an answer. He scratched at the back of his head, his expression almost embarrassed. "The Water mage asked for suggestions. He didn't know what to do today."

"And you made this happen? So many lives were changed today. How did you know he could even do that?"

He sighed. "If I had his powers, no one would ever hurt again. But I don't, so I did what I could. I wasn't sure he could do it. He wasn't either. We thought he'd manage a few—his parents are both Healers, so his lineage is quite strong—but I had no idea he'd be able to do that."

"It was incredible," Ros said.

Cassian nodded. "I don't want credit for his work, Princess. That's not why I took you to see them."

"Then why?"

"Because you need to know your people."

Ros felt heat rise up her throat. "I *know* my people."

Cassian smirked, sending anger bubbling through Ros. He said, "Don't take it personally. Most Elementalists don't bother with the magicless, and royalty has a tendency to avoid them altogether. But the things we do affect them, too. Sometimes rulers just need to be reminded."

Ros realized she was still standing against him as they talked and she pulled away. "You have some nerve. Coming here with your little party trick, trying to guilt me about knowing my people. You know nothing about me."

"I know more than you think, *Rosa*."

Her breath nearly stopped. Only Alaric called her that, only he knew...

Cassian continued, "I know what it means to love you, to be broken by you, to receive only the tiniest shred of emotion that you return. But at least you've known a magicless person as more than a servant, even if it was only for your amusement."

The shadow in her room last night, the one she saw moving after she'd made Alaric leave... It was *him*.

When she didn't respond, Cassian added, "And I can do more than a little party trick, Your Highness."

His hands stretched out and dark swirls rose from all around them. They stretched up and out over the stadium, filling it in darkness. He turned to look at her and signaled a finger above them. As he did, a single star shone in the spot where he pointed. He jerked out his other hand and gestured to the side where another star emerged. He moved his hands faster and faster until there was a whole galaxy above them.

She looked up, unable to hide the awe on her face. Almost as soon as he saw her expression, the stars disappeared. The darkness above began to crack, letting seams of light shine through. The shadowed sky splintered open and the darkness returned to swirls that spiraled back down to him. They pooled under his and Rosalinde's feet, lifting them higher and higher into the night.

The shadows dropped out from under them and they were falling. Ros screamed, true terror filling her as the ground grew closer. At the last second, she felt Cassian's arm slip around her waist and the next moment, they were back in the royal box.

"I can be stealthy," he said, but his face showed no hint of joking. His eyes grew darker still, almost completely black as he growled, "You hear me when I want you to hear me. You see what I want you to see. I am not one of these boys here to impress you with silliness, Rosalinde. I hold true power, the likes of which you've never seen. This *performance* is just that, a show for the people around us. But I can show you my strength. I can teach you how to tap into something so much bigger than everything you know about the Elements. Do you crave that kind of power, Princess?"

She stared at him in stunned silence, unsure how much time passed between them. There was nothing she could say, nothing to quench the fear inside her as she searched those black eyes for a hint of the man he'd been just minutes before.

Finally, she managed to find her spirit again, saying, "I want nothing to do with you or the power you claim to have. I don't need that to be a good queen."

"What do you need, Rosalinde?"

"Heart. And I have more than enough of that."

Without another word, he disappeared from the box and reappeared in the center of the arena, smiling and waving to the crowd. They cheered for him, whether from the things he had done or the healed people spreading the story of how he had come to them, how he had saved them.

Rosalinde's shaking hand went to the paper with his name on it. She gave him the lowest score possible. She wanted to tell him to leave now, to go back to the nothing he came from and never return. But she couldn't, not with the way the commonfolk adored him. Still, she could rate him low in every event, make it clear she had no interest in him, and chase away his favor with the townsfolk.

She had to. After his display today, she knew any kindness he had shown was false. He was dark-hearted, callous, and manipulative. Worst of all, if he hadn't let his mask fall and shown her who he truly was, she probably would have considered him as one of the top contenders.

Ros had thought he was handsome, mysterious, and a little bit dangerous; now though, his features looked sour and the mystery had revealed a cruel man.

The dangerous part—that was real.

But Rosalinde Managold could be dangerous, too.

Eight

Outside was dark, but the castle was ablaze with light shining from every window. Rosalinde's hands were still shaking when she stepped back inside. Though she'd been escorted by a dozen guards, and despite her own elemental potency, she still felt disturbingly inadequate compared to the Night mage. The control he exhibited over darkness was more than she had anticipated.

Cassian's powers didn't seem violent, but they were still menacing. And his temperament seemed fickle and unknowable. If he desired to be good, he could use his gift to rescue people from death's grasp. But if his mood shifted, what might he do? Based on what she'd seen at his demonstration, he could capture his victim from anywhere, taking them any place he wanted, and they were powerless to defend themselves. And what could guards do against a shadow, a wisp of darkness?

Ros shivered, despite the warmth of the castle. She couldn't let her mind dwell on Cassian, not when there was so much else to think about. She'd spent her day being the dutiful princess, keeping her focus, and being who they needed her to be. Now that she was home, she was ready to just be a daughter again, desperate to know what was going on with her mother and father.

She passed the dining hall. Glancing in, she could see it was already filling up with hungry mages and guests. She didn't have time to stay, despite the way her stomach growled at the aroma wafting from the nearby kitchens.

Ros turned the corner to sneak up the servants' passage to the royal chambers, hopefully bypassing curious noble eyes. She'd only taken one step when she heard someone yell her name. She paused, wondering how far she could make it before whoever it was caught up to her, but no, it was already too late.

Zandor came into view at the edge of the passage, propping his arm against the door frame. "You're not coming to dinner? Won't the judges be announcing the scores?"

Ros took a step back down, closing the gap between them. She whispered, "I'll be there as soon as I can. I need to find my parents."

"I'm sure they'll be along shortly."

Zandor's sister, Larkin, ducked her head under his arm and stepped into the staircase entrance. "There you are. I've been trying to catch up to you but the crowd was wild and there were guards everywhere." She took one look at Rosalinde's face and added, "What's wrong?"

Ros shook her head, unsure how much she should tell them. "Nothing. Everything's fine."

"You're a terrible liar, babe. Did my fool of a brother—"

"I didn't do anything," Zandor said.

Larkin took Rosalinde's hand in her own and asked, "What's wrong, love?"

Ros felt a sob rise in her throat and fought to hold it back. She choked out the words, "The last I heard, my father was…misplaced. Mother was too distraught to stay for the performance today, so Elsa escorted her back to the castle."

Larkin's gaze softened. "You were alone for the opening ceremony? I'm so sorry."

"It's fine," Ros said, swallowing back the emotion fighting its way into her tone. "I need to find out what's going on and if my father is still missing."

"Missing?" Zandor asked, his voice pitching high.

Ros shushed him and said, "Please, keep this between us. I don't need the whole palace in an uproar because the king is missing."

Florian's face sprang into view behind Zandor. "The king is missing?"

As soon as the words left Florian's lips, she could hear them move down the hall like a river of gossip. Panicked voices echoed the words and Rosalinde knew she would need to address the people before she could go any farther.

She looked at the siblings and sighed. "I'll have to take care of this."

"Sorry," Zandor muttered.

"I'll go find your mom," Larkin said.

Ros nodded. To Zandor, she said, "Lord Zolto, would you be so kind as to escort me to the great hall?"

Zandor held out his arm and she took it, letting him push their way through the concerned guests. She went to her place at the table, but with everyone milling around and talking about the missing king, no one noticed she was prepared to speak.

Graeme cut through the room, his wind moving ahead of him to push people out of his way. Jostled mages turned to protest against his forcefulness, but he paid them no mind, keeping his eyes on Rosalinde. When he reached her, he said, "I just heard about the king. Is it true?"

Ros pressed her lips together and nodded. "I came to address the assembly, but they're so distracted that they have yet to notice me."

"I can help with that," Graeme said.

He held out his hand and Ros took it. She felt a breeze pick up around them and then they were levitating above the table on wings of air. Those closest stopped talking, distracted by the floating princess in their midst. Soon the entire room had quieted down and all eyes were on her.

Ros said, "Esteemed guests, as you've all recently heard, my father is missing. I'm certain everything is fine and there's nothing to worry about, but as soon as I have more information, I'll let you know."

"Is that why he wasn't at the opening ceremony?" someone yelled.

She winced, unsure what to say. At this point, she needed to assuage their fears without diminishing the significance of what was happening. More importantly, she didn't want to lie and make things worse.

"My father loves our yearly celebration in all its forms. He was likely caught up in some other form of entertainment for the afternoon. Again, I'm still waiting for further information."

"Speak plainly, Princess."

Rosalinde looked toward the man who spoke to her, the crowd parting before him as he moved toward the table. Her knees shook as she watched him approach, knowing whatever happened next would define this whole event. Hessian Barclay, the Lord Ruler of Air House and her father's most outspoken rival, would undoubtedly find a way to use this moment.

"What would you have me say, good Lord?" Rosalinde asked, drawing herself to her full height. "I do not wish to cause worry when my father could walk in at any moment. Until I have more news of what has happened today, the conversation is at a standstill."

A fresh gust of wind lifted Hessian so he was face to face with Ros. Though he would never be so brazen with her father, his absence seemed to have allowed the man to grow emboldened.

"I appreciate your desire to keep things calm. But the people gathered here are not the magicless herd you're accustomed to. We desire, nay, we *demand* the truth," he said, his voice carrying through the room. "Could there have been foul play?"

Whispers surged at his words. From the edge of the room, Florian called out, "We all saw what the Night mage can do. If anyone's to blame, I'd bet it's him."

Ros tried to block out the words, the sense it made. It wasn't as if she hadn't already considered it. He had the ability, and even if he didn't have a motive, perhaps his mother still held a grudge. But she knew where he'd been that morning when her father went missing. The townsfolk could clear his name.

"It wouldn't be the first time your father had trouble with a Night mage," Hessian said, his eyes narrowing as he looked across the room to Cassian.

Ros looked to Cassian, expecting a denial or an alibi at least. Instead, he took a bite of a bright red apple, his expression wholly unconcerned.

"He doesn't bother denying it," Hessian declared. "Princess, what are you going to do with this fiend?"

Ros felt her cheeks burn as people turned accusing eyes between her and Cassian. She said, "There's no reason to assume the Night Lord has anything to do with this. As I've told you—"

"You haven't told us anything," he said.

The crowd grew more reckless with the Air house Lord's words. Now that they had a leader to step behind, they would all soon back him unless she could squash it right now.

Despite years of training urging her to do the opposite, Rosalinde let her anger rise, bidding it to fuel her gift. She felt the familiar surge of power as the magic in her veins began to burst from her. Water dripped down her body now, pouring from her skin. Her hair and dress were soaked through in an instant and she let a tsunami build under her feet.

Graeme and his wind fell away. She didn't need him, not when her own gifts could raise her as high as she wished. And she let it. The wave lifted her above the Air Lord, higher into the room until she could turn and see every person, every horrified face as she looked down on them.

Her voice boomed through the room: "Do not question the House of Water, my Lord, or you will find yourself ill-equipped to handle the reply."

She felt the power surging below her, begging for release. She could drown the lot of them, if she wished. Part of her did. The dark part of her, the side she kept locked away, the reason she never used her powers. She felt that secret portion of her fighting for control even now.

Her eyes trailed from one face to the next, though

none would meet her gaze. Even Hessian had lowered himself back to the ground. Though he wore a mask of calm, she knew she had only distracted him from his goal. He would come for her house again, her throne.

It would be so easy to kill him now. To let the water flood over him. She could control it and everyone else would be safe. She closed her eyes and raised her hands. She could...

"Still your storm, friend."

The voice was calm and easy, deeper than when she'd last heard it, but she recognized Brensen's words as if she'd heard him only yesterday.

"I can't," she growled through clenched teeth.

"Of course you can. You're the scion of Water house, the future of your noble name. You can do anything. Now recede the waters, Rosalinde."

He grasped her shoulders with both of his hands. Her eyes shot open, shocked that he would grab her like that in front of the other guests. "You dare—"

Dark eyes met hers. Though Brensen stood at her side trying to calm her, it was the Night mage whose hands rested on her bare skin. His voice was gentle as he said, "Let me help you."

She stared into his eyes as he held her in place. A jolt passed through her, lurching her toward him, and she felt the dark part of herself seep away. Slowly at first, but then urgently, as if it couldn't wait to get out of her.

Rosalinde took a deep breath. She hadn't noticed the tightness in her lungs, the pressure on her chest, but now that it was gone she wasn't sure if she'd even been breathing. The water receded below her feet, leaving her drenched and embarrassed as she stood in the middle of the room.

A path had been cleared around her, and though Hessian Barclay had ceased his questions, Ros couldn't help but feel she'd made things far worse. She glanced throughout the room, noting the wide-eyed terror on some of their faces. This was why she wasn't supposed to call on her magic. It was too dangerous, too wild and uncontrollable, and now so many of them had seen it.

She looked to Cassian at her side; his was the only gaze that did not show fear. She whispered, "Get me out of here."

She felt his fingers at her wrist and the room disappeared.

THEY STOOD in her chambers near the window. For a moment, she simply stared at him, forgetting the chaos of everything going on around her. She wasn't sure what she was looking for, but she needed *something* from him. Was he the stranger smirking after she fell, the clever man making her laugh through breakfast, the dark shadow lurking around every corner? Or was he all of these things, and maybe something more that she had yet to define? She'd been ready to rule him out a quarter of an hour ago at the opening ceremony, and yet he had been the one to save her—and the other Elementalists—from herself.

His eyes met hers only briefly before he turned his face away and cleared his throat. "I thought perhaps your family would be in a nearby room."

She inhaled sharply as everything came back to her. Without a word, Ros darted from the room. She went to Elsabet's chambers, but there was no one inside. Her mother's room was next, but again there was no one.

Ros stopped in front of her father's door, placing her hand against the gleaming gold filigree. So strange a thing, the designs of swooping birds and flowers and trees, when there was a water mage who resided there. She took in every detail of the door, despite ignoring it for years. As long as she didn't open it, as long as she didn't go inside, her father could be there and everything could be fine. But the moment she opened it...

A hand covered hers against the door. She looked up to see Cassian at her side yet again. But for the first time, his face was unreadable. He said, "Open the door, Rosalinde."

Ros swallowed, shook her head. "I can't."

He nodded, seeming to understand. A moment later, they were in the stables. Ros looked around as if she didn't recognize the place. She had spent her fair share of time there throughout the years, having clandestine meetings with her secret and short-lived beaus, but it had been awhile since she'd been back. Though nothing seemed to have changed, everything looked different.

Cassian took a couple steps toward one of the stalls. Unsure what else to do, Ros followed. Inside the stall was a gorgeous horse with a pale gold coat and a brilliant white mane and tail. It whinnied when Cassian approached, nuzzling his hand when he held it forward.

Ros watched them for several minutes as Cassian whispered sweetly to the beast, stroking its fur and feeding it sugar cubes that he seemed to draw from nowhere.

Finally, he looked up and upon seeing Ros, seemed startled. He smiled sheepishly at her and said, "This is Desdemona."

"What a horrible name," Ros said, reaching forward. "It means 'unlucky,' you know."

Desdemona snapped at Rosalinde's hand. She drew it back as Cassian barked a laugh. "Oh, I know. She's a horrible old thing. Hates almost everyone."

"Not you."

"Well, that's because I help her when the darkness comes."

Ros looked over at him, but he kept his eyes on Desdemona. She asked, "The darkness?"

"You know what I'm talking about, Princess."

She did. She'd felt it consuming her only moments ago, and it was Cassian who had come to her rescue. "What is it exactly?"

Cassian shrugged. "I don't know, really. But it's in everything that lives. Sometimes it's just a small bit, easy to ignore. Other times, it's stronger and harder to control. For a long time, I thought it had to do with the strength of magic and that people with stronger gifts had it worse. But then I've met some magicless who had to fight each day to keep the darkness at bay. Even poor darlings like Desi here have to fight it."

"I thought it was just me. I thought I was broken."

"No, not at all," he said, running his hand over Desi's mane. "Do you want to talk about what happened in the dining hall?"

Ros bit her lip. "Not really."

He nodded, not pressing her further. After a moment of silence, Ros asked, "How did you do it? How did you take the darkness from me?"

"I didn't take it away. I just tempered it and absorbed the excess."

That hadn't been what she was hoping for. Ros had wanted him to tell her it was gone and would never return. But he didn't.

He looked at her then, and on his face was something she hadn't yet seen: compassion. He turned quickly, hiding his expression as he moved to the next stall. "I'm sorry. I'd take it from you if I could, so that it wouldn't haunt you again."

"Does it haunt you, too?"

For a moment, she thought he wouldn't answer, but finally he said, "It can't haunt me for long, even if it wanted to. I specialize in darkness, Princess."

"Ros," she said. "That's what my friends call me."

"Are we friends now? I was certain you would despise me, after today."

"Despise? You just saved me from unleashing a tsunami on the Lords and Ladies of the Elemental Houses."

He grimaced. "Before that. At the opening ceremony."

She chewed on the inside of her cheek for a second, contemplating his words. "Right, that. I wasn't happy with you, that's for sure."

Cassian laughed so hard he nearly choked. "Come now, Princess. I know what hate looks like. You're not the first woman to stare at me as if she wanted to murder me."

"While I'm not at all surprised to hear that women hate you, I am surprised that it is *only* women who hate you. I have seen the effect you have on Florian, after all."

Cassian lifted a hand to cover his heart, his face taking on an anguished look. "You wound me so. The Fire lad and I are firm friends."

She swatted his arm as he reached in to stroke the mane of a horse the color of night, as black as the darkest part of Ros. Though her eyes were on the lovely creature, she found herself thinking about the way Cassian's temperament had changed so drastically earlier and how he had avoided her question about the darkness haunting him. She said, "You didn't answer my question. About the darkness, I mean."

A pause before he said, "No, I didn't."

"Will you?"

"Not willingly."

"And if I command you?"

"Then I would be forced to give you my secrets, but not my trust."

"I would like to have your trust," she said, turning to look at him.

He stared down at her for a long moment before saying, "And I would like to give it. Prove to me that you deserve it, Ros."

She moved past him to the next stall where a white horse with black splotches whinnied at her approach. She reached forward and stroked the beast's neck, then scratched behind his ear. When she glanced at Cassian, he was watching her with a bemused smile.

"What?" she asked.

"Nothing," he said, scrubbing a hand over his short, black hair. "It's just, Mercutio doesn't normally like people to touch him."

"Are all of your horses as antisocial as you?"

He laughed. "I'm not antisocial. I just take time to warm up. Besides, most people aren't worth the time it takes to get to know them."

"How do you know that if you never try?"

"I've tried," he said, his eyes going sad.

"They're afraid of you," Ros whispered.

He nodded. "Usually, yeah. Comes with the territory of controlling shadows. People are afraid of the dark, Ros. But you don't seem to be."

"I was earlier."

The confession seemed to take him off guard and for a moment she wished she could take it back. The truth, though, was that he did frighten her. His gift, his shift in mood, but also, the way her very soul seemed to calm in his presence. That was the part that frightened her most.

"I'm sorry for what I said at the ceremony." He fidgeted with the cuff of his sleeve as if the idea of apologizing made him nervous. In a soft voice, he added, "There's darkness in me, too, Ros. I can usually control it, but when it comes out, it's ugly. I regret that you saw that part of me."

Ros wondered at the way he spoke about the darkness as if it was a tangible thing. Perhaps it was for someone who could control it. She looked at him, at the way he seemed so vulnerable and kind to her now, and she wondered if this was the part of him that was real. Though she hoped to keep this version of Cassian with her, she couldn't let go of the other one in her mind, the one who was dangerous.

"I have to ask you something," she said, swallowing hard. "But I don't want to anger you."

Cassian met her eyes and said, "I didn't kidnap your father. I don't know what has become of him."

"How did you know that was my question?"

He shrugged. "It's what I would have asked, were I in your shoes. A stranger comes to your home using the gifts I have, and the King of Talabrih suddenly goes missing? The irony isn't lost on me."

"He may be fine."

Cassian nodded. "Maybe. Why didn't you check?"

She sighed. "Once I open that door, there's no going back. I have to face whatever or whoever is on the other side."

"You can't move forward until you do."

"I know. I just needed a minute to prepare."

"Take as long as you need, Princess. I am at your disposal. Until the angry mob thinks I've kidnapped you, too. Then we might need to return."

Ros smiled at that. Though truthfully, it probably wasn't far from possible. They stood there for a long moment in silence, Ros running her hand along Mercutio's coat while Cassian watched in silence. When Rosalinde's heart finally eased its frantic beating and she felt mostly normal, she said, "Okay, I'm ready to go back. Can't have you accused of two kidnappings today."

"I'm already the frontrunner in one royal disappearance, but two seems like too much, even for me."

Cassian put his arm around her waist and took her other hand. When he'd done it before, it had felt strangely formal and stiff. Now though, there was an intimacy between them and Ros could feel a strange current running from each placement of his fingers. She was surprised to discover that she welcomed his touch.

They stepped through the streams of light until they stood in front of her father's door. Rosalinde felt Cassian's warmth recede. She wanted to pull him back to her as soon as he stepped away, but she knew that was probably a bad idea. They hardly knew one another, and though she felt a strange connectedness to him right now after only a few minutes alone in the stables, her head was clear enough to realize it was probably due more to circumstance than actual feelings.

So instead of reaching for him, she put on her bravest face and pushed against the door.

Nine

The room was a flurry of activity. There were servants carrying messages, food, and writing supplies throughout the room. Guards moved between tables covered in maps as they called things back and forth to one another. It was precise chaos.

In the center was Queen Sariyah. Her dark hair was pulled back into a braid, her gown gone, replaced by a black pantsuit similar to the one the competitors wore in the Match. She pored over maps and answered questions, commanded guards and servants who brought her things.

Ros headed straight for her. "Mother, what's going on?"

"Ah, Rosalinde," she said when she caught sight of her. "I suppose Larkin found you?"

"What? No."

"I asked her to bring you to me." Sariyah waved her

hand and said, "Never mind that. How was the opening ceremony?"

"Fine," she said, waving away the question. "Unimportant."

"Unimportant?" Sariyah asked. "This is the future of the kingdom we're talking about, love. Please tell me there's at least a few potential matches."

"Yes, fine, there are some, but my mind is far more focused on what's happening here. What exactly *is* happening here?"

The queen looked around as if the answer should be obvious. "We're trying to find the King, Rosalinde."

"He's still missing? I thought maybe..."

"He wouldn't have missed the opening ceremony under any circumstances, darling. The Great Match is too important to him. *You* are important to him. More than anything else that might have come up. If he's gone..." she trailed off, brows furrowing.

"Then you suspect he didn't leave on his own."

"I've known that man for twenty-five years. There's no chance he left of his own accord."

"Your Highness," a guard called. "I found this man lurking outside the doors."

He dragged Cassian forward, though somehow the Night mage managed to look like he was simply out for a leisurely stroll. The queen stepped in front of him, her presence so commanding that Ros wasn't sure how Cassian didn't flinch.

Instead, his face held an easy smile as he bowed and

said, "Good evening, Your Majesty. Lovely to see you again."

"Why were you outside? Returning to the scene of the crime?"

"He's with me," Ros said, stepping between them.

The queen's eyebrow quirked up, her mouth parting slightly in surprise. "He's with *you*?"

Ros felt her cheeks color at the way her mother asked, but she held her ground. "Yes. He's a friend and he's here to help."

Cassian looked at her as if this was news to him, and Ros wasn't sure if his expression was due to calling him a friend or offering his help without consulting him.

Sariyah pressed two fingers to the bridge of her nose. "Rosalinde, please tell me you haven't already done something foolish, like choosing a husband after the opening ceremony."

Cassian barked a laugh, tried to turn it into a cough, but failed miserably. He said, "Her Highness can barely tolerate my presence, Your Majesty. Calling me a friend was a kindness of which I am not worthy. But she has agreed to let me be of service, if the need arises, and I am here in that capacity."

"Is that right?" Queen Sariyah asked, folding her arms across her chest.

Ros gave him a small apologetic shrug and the corner of his lip twitched up. He said, "I am at your disposal."

"I'll keep that in mind for when I need the candles

dimmed." She turned to Ros and asked, "How many of the Elementalists know the king is gone?"

"All of them."

Queen Sariyah tilted her head back and let out a frustrated sigh. "Okay, that's okay, we can still work with that." She waved the head guard over and said, "The other houses know he's missing. Let's start questioning them to see what we can learn."

As the guard left, Ros asked, "Do we have any leads?"

"Not yet. The most suspicious person is currently at your side," Sariyah said, glancing at Cassian. "But so far we haven't discovered any concrete evidence it was him."

"It wasn't," Ros said.

Sariyah pursed her lips and continued, "We searched the town while the people were at the opening ceremony—"

"You went through people's houses without their permission?" Cassian asked.

Sariyah sneered at him. "The ruler of the kingdom is missing. Privacy isn't high on my list of priorities right now."

Ros was surprised by her mother, but tried to steer the conversation back to what was most important. "When was he last seen?"

"We had breakfast together, then I went for a walk in the garden and he left for the medical unit," Sariyah said. "He wanted to check on a patient with some unusual symptoms that came in last night during dinner. A few people saw your father when he arrived at the clinic, but none saw him leave. We can't find any trace of him after that."

"Can we speak with the patient?"

The queen shook her head. "We sent guards there earlier, but the patient had already checked out."

"Can we survey the room?" Cassian asked.

"What room?" Ros asked.

"The one he went to visit."

"We checked the room. It's empty," the queen said.

"Still, I'd like to see it," Cassian said.

"Suit yourself," Sariyah said. "He was in room twenty-three."

Cassian nodded and asked, "Princess Rosalinde, would you be so kind as to show me to the medical unit? I'm unfamiliar with the layout of the castle."

Ros nodded, but the queen's eyes narrowed at the request. "On second thought, I'll send a guard with you, just in case."

As Ros and Cassian walked toward the door, a giant woman stepped behind them. Ros knew her, of course, and was glad the queen had chosen Romenia for the task. The woman was vicious with a blade and one of the strongest warriors Ros had ever seen. She knew her own magic was fierce and Cassian's gift could remove them from danger, but she still felt safer with Romenia's sword at their disposal.

After they were away from the queen, Ros asked, "Why didn't you just magic us to the medical unit?"

Cassian smirked. "It doesn't work that way."

"How does it work?"

"Can't a man have any mystery around you? Maybe I'd like to keep a few secrets, Princess."

"It seems to me you're made of secrets."

He sighed. "Okay, I'll give you this one: I need to be looking at the place I'm going to travel to, or be able to pull it up from a memory."

"Well, that confirms at least one thing."

"What's that?"

"You were in my bedroom last night." She paused for a few seconds before adding, "I knew, after what you said at the ceremony—I mean, you weren't exactly subtle. But part of me hoped it was a coincidence. It wasn't though, because you took us to my bedroom when we left the dining hall. So you were there last night, watching me say goodbye to Alaric. Watching me break his heart."

He winced. They took several steps in silence before he said, "I'm sorry about that. I didn't mean to see what I saw."

Ros bit the inside of her cheek. She felt like she should be angry, or maybe embarrassed, but she didn't feel either. "Why were you there?"

"I couldn't sleep and I was wandering the castle. I saw a man walking toward the royal apartments and wanted to know why. I didn't know it was your room I was entering until it was too late."

"He could've been a servant, or a messenger, or even another guest."

"He wasn't in house colors," Cassian said. "Nor did he look like any of the other guests."

"That doesn't excuse you for entering my chambers as you did."

"I know. I wanted to leave straight away, but I was afraid you'd see me. And then when I realized what was happening, well, I was curious. It was a chance to see the real you without the weight of the crown on your head. Everything about you surprised me. The gentleness, the weight of the moment clear upon your face, the love you have for that man..."

"You are mistaken," she whispered. "I don't love him. I sent him away."

"You lied to him, Ros, but you cannot lie to me. Nor should you have to. What crime is there in loving a magicless person?"

"You are a contender for the right to be my husband, yet it doesn't bother you that I have recently loved someone else?"

Cassian shook his head. "Sometimes I wonder if Talabrih's nobility is capable of love. But then I saw it in you. I would be lucky for a chance to work for that love."

"Our kingdom isn't built on love," Ros said. "It's built on agreements, partnerships."

"Wouldn't it be nice if it could be more?"

The patter of their footfalls echoed around them for a few moments while neither of them spoke. Finally, Cassian asked, "Who is he, anyway?"

"A good man."

"Better that you sent him away then. Our world is no place for good men."

"Are you not a good man?"

Cassian's smirk tilted up and he said, "I'm the sort who sneaks into your bedroom at night."

"Maybe that's the sort I prefer."

He smiled then, but it didn't last long. "I am truly sorry for that intrusion. It's inexcusable, unforgivable. Honestly, I'm surprised you haven't sent me away for that."

"I can't send you away," Ros said. "Not until the end of the week."

Ros glanced over, trying to read his face, but he wouldn't look at her. They continued on wordlessly, but Ros felt a pang of regret that the conversation had turned the way it had. Cassian had opened up and shared a secret of his gift, something no one else knew about him and the Night house, but the moment had turned into something much different.

He should know that she was displeased with him. There was no excuse for him to have entered her room as he did, no matter his intentions. but she didn't want him to close off from her when she was just getting to know him. Still, she wasn't sure how to get back to the moment before. And she wasn't sure why it mattered so much to her.

THEY MADE their way through the back halls to avoid the other mages. This area was less ornate, with simpler decorations and far less gilding. Ros preferred this part of the castle. It wasn't showy, didn't try to impress, while still remaining solid. She glanced to Cassian at her side. Maybe that's what she liked about the Night Elementalist, too.

Ros rolled her eyes at her own thoughts. Of all the things she could be thinking right now, that should not have made it to the surface of her mind. How had he managed to shift her thoughts to him despite the bad things he had done? Besides, even if she could forgive his behavior, which she couldn't, he was not the sort of man she could choose even if she wanted to. His magic was too frightening, his element too taboo for him to be accepted as the future king of Talabrih. And he himself had said he wasn't a good man. That told Ros all she needed to know.

They stepped into the stone-gray halls of the medical unit. Ros greeted a young healer she knew as they passed. "Evening, Elaina."

"Princess," she said, bowing her head. "I'm so sorry to hear about your father."

Ros was a bit surprised the talk had made it this far, but then again, servants and guards had been in and out of her mother's war room all afternoon. It would be impossible to keep things quiet for long.

"Thank you," Ros said. "That's why we're here. We're going to the last place anyone saw him."

"Twenty-three," Elaina said with a shiver. "I knew that patient was bad news."

"You saw the patient?" Cassian asked. "Could you describe them?"

Elaina nodded. She opened her mouth to speak, but her eyes rolled back in her head and her body convulsed. She stumbled and Romenia caught her, lifting the healer into her strong arms.

"We need a Healer," Cassian yelled.

A few doors down, Teague stepped into the hall. His hair was mussed, like he'd been sleeping, and he still wore his uniform from the Great Match. Dark bruises had formed under his eyes and there was a weariness to him that Ros had never seen before.

He saw Elaina's prone form and his entire demeanor changed from the tired young man to a seasoned medic. "Bring her here."

Romenia carried Elaina to Teague's room and placed her on the bed. "What happened?"

"We were just talking," Cassian said.

As they stepped inside, Ros was surprised to see that Teague wasn't alone. The Botanical mage, Beckett, was sitting in a chair in the corner. He jumped up and bowed stiffly when he saw Ros.

"None of that," she said, stepping toward the wall beside him while Teague inspected Elaina. "Checking on our Healer?"

"Yes," he said, forcing a smile.

"I didn't know you were friends."

Beckett's face softened at the words, as if Ros had struck on something that made him joyful and wistful at the same time. "We are. Teague and I are very close. I was quite concerned after his display this afternoon."

"It *was* something," Ros muttered.

"I don't get it," Teague said, cutting off their conversation.

"What's wrong?" Cassian asked.

"She's not responding to healing."

"She's stopped convulsing," Ros said.

Teague waved a hand and said, "Her body stopped on its own."

"Maybe you're not recovered from earlier," Beckett said. "We could call for another Healer."

"I'm fine," Teague snapped. He ran a hand through his hair and heaved a sigh. "Sorry, Beck. It's just, I can feel the magic. I know it's working on my side. But Elaina's body is rejecting it."

"Can I try?" Cassian asked.

"Try what?" Teague asked.

"Healing."

Teague's brows rose toward his hairline. "There's no such thing as a Night house Healer. Not in the history of all of Talabrih."

Cassian shrugged. "Can't hurt."

"Any objections, Your Highness?"

Ros shook her head. "This is your domain, Teague. I trust your judgment."

"It's highly irregular, but I saw Cassian's compassion

earlier today when he helped me at the opening ceremony. I trust him."

Teague stepped aside and Cassian moved beside the bed. He put his hands out like Teague had done, hovering inches above Elaina's chest. Ros stepped forward to see what he was doing. She'd watched people using the Healing gift since she was a child, but they were all from Water house. Seeing someone from another house trying to heal felt strange, almost blasphemous.

She stepped up beside him and whispered, "What are you doing?"

Eyes closed, he smiled and said, "I don't know. I'm going with my gut."

"Your gut says you're a Healer now?"

"My gut says there's a connection between all this. Your dad's disappearance, the strange patient, Elaina's reaction when she was about to tell us about him. I just have to find the link."

"Can I help?"

He opened his mouth to answer, but instead tilted his head to the side. "I think I've found something."

Ros watched as Cassian's fingers twitched over Elaina's body. Seconds passed while the room held a collective breath. A tendril of black smoke curled up from Elaina's chest. Cassian moved his fingers as if to beckon it out of her and the smoke followed as he directed.

Romenia's hand covered her mouth and she gasped, "Dear gods, what is that?"

But the only person who might be able to answer her was focused on pulling it out of Elaina. As the wisp of darkness left her body, it curled around Cassian's hand and dissolved into his skin.

Cassian stumbled back away from the girl and out the door. Ros looked to Teague and said, "Try now," before following Cassian into the hallway. He was doubled over with his hands on his knees, gulping in air like he couldn't get enough.

Ros put her hand on his shoulder and said, "What can I do?"

Cassian jerked up at her touch and lunged at her, pushing her against the wall. He pinned her arms above her head, holding her in place with his body. Ros felt terror rise in her chest as she stared into his eyes. They were that terrifying empty black she had seen before, and she knew the darkness had taken him.

Ten

"Look at me," she said, her voice shaking.

Cassian's eyes roamed up and down her body as his mouth twisted in a wicked smile. He licked his lips and said, "Oh, I'm looking. I'm seeing it all."

"Cassian, please," she said. "This isn't you."

At least, she thought it wasn't. She'd seen a different part of him every time they interacted, but there was a good part of him that she thought was the real Cassian, and she couldn't believe this thing in front of her was the same person.

He leaned down until his lips brushed her ear. Slowly, so slowly it sent a shiver over her body, he whispered, "You don't know *me*, Princess. You've imagined another side of me to fit your narrative, to make me redeemable in your eyes, but this is the real me."

He ran his tongue up her neck and nipped at her ear.

She squirmed against him and he growled out a laugh. He pulled back and looked down at her, his face contorted into someone she didn't recognize. "Don't pretend you don't want this. I've felt the hunger in you."

"You have to fight this. You have to come back to me," she whispered.

He winced at her words, his cruel expression breaking for just a second. Ros felt his grip around her wrists loosen. She could see flashes of the real Cassian between sneers and growls. Little by little, he was coming out of it.

"What the hell?"

Rosalinde's head snapped toward Larkin's voice at the same second a blur of motion tackled Cassian away from her. Zandor and Cassian rolled across the floor, grappling as arms swung at one another.

Larkin ran to her side. "Are you okay? Did he hurt you?"

"I'm fine," Ros said. "It's not what it looked like."

"He had you pinned against the wall, Ros. Don't make excuses for him."

"Please, trust me. I'll explain everything. Just help me get them apart."

The men were still scrapping and Ros wasn't sure who was winning, if either of them. Larkin shrugged, unsure how to help. Ros took a deep breath and focused on her power. She didn't need a tsunami, just a spray of water, and she couldn't let it overwhelm her like before.

Water dripped at her hairline as she stretched out her

hand and released a jet of saltwater at the two men. They fell apart, rubbing the sting from their eyes as they struggled against the barrage.

She felt Larkin's hand on her shoulder and heard her say, "That's enough."

Ros felt the shadow at the edge of her power pushing her to give more, more, more. She reined it in, fighting that part of her and letting the magic fall away until there was only a trickle coming from her index finger. Cassian stood, his clothes dripping wet, a glorious smile on his face.

"Brilliant, Ros, absolutely brilliant."

"Um, no, you don't get to talk to her until you explain why you had her pinned against the wall," Larkin said, stepping between them.

Zandor joined Larkin's side, wiping water from his face. He gave Ros a hurt look and she couldn't tell if it was from the fact that she'd doused him with water or what he'd seen when he walked in.

Before anyone could say anything, Beckett stuck his head out into the hallway. Confusion crossed his face as he took in the soaked men and palpable tension. He hooked his thumb over his shoulder and said, "Yeah, I don't know what I missed out here, but Elaina's awake."

Cassian stepped toward the door, but Zandor put a hand on his chest and said, "Don't think this is over."

Cassian quirked up a smile at him as he slipped past. He grabbed Rosalinde's hand and pulled her into Elaina's room. Zandor and Larkin followed them in just as Teague said, "I don't know what you did, but it saved her life. As soon as you got that stuff out of her, she was able to receive the healing."

They stepped to her side and Cassian asked, "Elaina, what can you tell us about the patient King Tancred came to see?"

Elaina squinted up at them, shaking her head. "King Tancred? He sees a lot of patients. Which one do you want to know about?"

"The one he came to see before he disappeared," Ros said.

"Disappeared?" she asked. "The king is missing?"

Teague said, "It could be a side effect of the trauma she experienced."

"Or whoever did this to her doesn't want to be remembered," Cassian said.

"You think someone did this *to* her?" Teague asked.

Cassian nodded. "It wasn't natural. At least not like anything natural I've ever seen."

"And you've seen everything, have you?" Zandor asked.

Cassian rounded on him and said, "You weren't here when it came out of her, so you can kindly drop the attitude, friend. And no, I haven't 'seen everything.' I *have* seen enough darkness to know what is naturally part of a person and what is magic."

"Wait," Larkin said. "What came out of her?"

Ros met her eyes. "Darkness. A swirl of it came out of her and went into Cassian."

Teague asked, "How did you handle it when she couldn't?"

"I've practiced controlling darkness since I was a child, so it doesn't affect me as strongly. I was able to absorb what was in her, but even with my gift, it was out of my control." His gaze turned to Ros and he said, "I am so sorry you had to see that, that you endured it."

Ros nodded. "It wasn't you. I knew that."

"What we saw in the hallway was a reaction from absorbing bad magic?" Larkin asked.

Cassian nodded, but his eyes stayed on Ros. "I can't apologize enough. I would never hurt you. Never. But the darkness..."

"Say no more," Ros said. "You're forgiven."

There was silence for a moment while the situation seemed to sink in to everyone. Finally, Zandor said, "Your mother said you were inspecting the room where your father was last seen. How did that turn into all this?"

"We were on our way there when we bumped into Elaina. She was going to tell us about the patient Father was visiting, but as soon as she tried, she went into convulsions. And now she can't seem to tell us anything."

"After the Night mage did some magic on her. Convenient," Zandor said.

Teague spoke up. "I'll vouch for Cassian, if need be. I couldn't help Elaina. I have no idea what that thing was or if any of our Healers could have helped her. If he hadn't been here, she could be dead right now."

"Or maybe he was the patient and he used some dark magic to keep her quiet," Zandor said.

Cassian rolled his eyes, but it was Teague who spoke. "He wasn't the patient. I know that without a doubt."

"How could you possibly know that? Weren't you getting ready for the opening ceremony when the King went missing?"

"I was," Teague said, "and Cassian was with me."

"What do you mean he was with you?" Beckett asked.

Ros looked between the two men. Beckett was clearly waiting for an explanation while Teague looked terrified to give one. She said, "He helped you set up the healings, right?"

Teague nodded, seemingly grateful for someone else supplying the words. "I was struggling to come up with a way to show my gift. Healing isn't glamorous."

"It's important though," Ros said.

"Of course. But how do you show a crowd of people a gift that isn't showy like the others?" He put his hand on Cassian's shoulder and said, "And that's where he came in. After breakfast, we visited the village and made plans. We were together until the ceremony started."

"He could've bewitched someone. Or maybe he has an accomplice," Zandor countered.

Cassian threw his hands in the air. "I realize you're dead-set on making me the villain here, but I'm trying to help. So, you can keep accusing me, or you can throw in with us and help solve this mystery."

"I don't care what role you fill as long as Ros is safe, and I don't think she will be if you're around."

The two men squared off in the small room, all clenched jaws and balled fists. Zandor had a few inches on Cassian, but Ros had a feeling if it came to a physical confrontation, Cassian would fight dirty. Still, she didn't want to see the results of their egotistical engagement.

She edged her way between them and said, "We don't have time for this. We came here to survey the room my father was in, and that's where we're going now. Either calm down and come with us or return to the main castle."

Zandor took a step back from her as if he'd been slapped. It only took her a second to realize it was from her words: *we* came here, *we're* going. Without thinking about it, she'd put herself on Cassian's side of the argument.

She glanced at Cassian and saw that he must've noticed, too. The corners of his perfect mouth were turned up in a delicious, victorious smile.

Rosalinde let Cassian and Teague, followed closely by Zandor, lead the way to the room where the mystery patient had been. Ros commanded Romenia to stay with Larkin and Elaina while she and Beckett trailed the others. She had to put some distance between herself and the Night mage. She didn't *want* distance between them, which is exactly how she knew she needed it.

Ros had fallen for the wrong man more times than she could count. Usually it wasn't serious: a crush on someone who conveniently forgot to mention he was betrothed, stolen kisses behind the barn with a boy who couldn't keep a secret, too many nights with Alaric when she knew she couldn't truly have him. But this was different. If she let herself fall for the wrong man, especially on the first day of the Great Match, she could end up choosing a bad husband and worse, a bad king.

Out of habit, she took Beckett's arm while they walked down the hall. He'd been quiet since learning that Cassian and Teague had spent the morning together. Still, she saw the way Beckett kept stealing glances of Teague. She knew that look, and though she didn't want to force anything out of him, she felt she deserved to know what was going on with two men who could potentially become her husband.

Rather than try to tease the information out of him, she decided not to mince words, asking, "How long have you been seeing Teague?"

"Just a few months," Beckett said.

Ros smiled as realization dawned on his face. He clearly hadn't meant to tell her, but had been too distracted to grasp what he was saying. His expression turned to horror, as if he was afraid of her response, and she suddenly felt horribly guilty for asking something so personal.

She placed the tips of her fingers on his forearm and said, "Your secret is safe with me, if that's what you're worried about. Though I'm not sure why you want to keep it secret. There's nothing to be ashamed of."

"If my father finds out—"

"He won't hear it from me, I assure you."

Beckett nodded. "He's so set on using me to climb the social ladder, he can't see that it's not what I want. I've tried to tell him, but it never ends well."

Though Ros couldn't remember much from his performance, she said, "You're a talented Elementalist. I'm sure you could find favor with my mother, without trying to marry into my family."

Beckett winced at those words, seeming to carry some guilt of his own. He said, "I'm sorry. I thought I'd be dismissed soon enough that you'd never have to know of my deception."

Ros said, "I'm no fool. I know this isn't a love match for me. But if *you* can have a love match with Teague, the most gifted Healer of our generation, why risk it by entering the games?"

"I didn't have a choice. My father entered me, prepared my set for today, planned out the entire week, really." Beckett smirked and said, "Two days from now, I'm supposed to woo you with my wit and charm. I've been practicing the script for months."

Ros smiled. "I'm sure I would have been putty in your hands. But you know I can't in good conscience choose you, right?"

He swallowed, his voice barely a whisper when he said, "I would be a good husband for you, Princess, and a king devoted to his people."

"I have no doubt. Still, you're in love with someone else."

His cheeks flushed. "I don't know if it's love..."

"Well," she said, "you deserve time to figure that out. At the end of the week, I'll request you to stay as my personal ambassador from Earth house. That should give your father some clout and give you a reason to stay close to Teague."

"But there's already an ambassador," he stammered.

Ros nodded. "For my father, yes, but someday I will choose my own. If I wish to have you stay on as a guest, I'm sure it could be arranged. And dear Teague will be here to help you get acquainted with castle life."

"You're not going to send us away?"

"Why would I send you away? Especially now that I know what an amazing Healer your boyfriend is. He'll be the next head of the medical unit, if I have any say."

A wide grin broke across Beckett's face and he beamed down at her. "You really are something, you know that? There's nothing I can ever do to repay you."

"I don't need payment for this or anything else. Just be happy. Don't waste time trying to hide something beautiful." She paused outside the room and said, "Actually, waste a little time. You'll still need to be part of the Great Match through the end of the week."

They stepped into the room where Cassian and

Teague were exploring every nook and cranny while Zandor watched them with unease. Ros knew he wanted to protect her, but his attitude was starting to piss her off. During all the years they'd been friends, she'd never seen him behave in such a way. This side of him was at odds with the man she knew and was pushing her farther away, reinforcing Larkin's advice not to choose him.

She stepped past him and asked, "Find anything?"

"No," Teague said at the same moment Cassian replied, "Maybe."

He pointed to the wall where there was a single bloody fingerprint. Teague said, "Might not belong to the king."

"Do the rooms get cleaned regularly?" Cassian asked, his finger hovering right above the blood.

"Of course," Teague bristled. "After every patient."

"And this patient has been gone for several hours. Why is it still there?"

Before Teague could find an answer, Cassian grabbed Ros by the hand and pulled her to the bloody print. He held her hand toward it, keeping her fingers only an inch above it.

"What are you doing?" she asked.

"Trying to see if there's a blood connection," Cassian said. "If I'm doing it right, and if the blood belongs to your father, we should see..."

He trailed off. He didn't need to say anything else. The blood on the wall was moving.

Ros watched the blood as it spun in a slow circle in

front of her fingertip. She asked, "How are you doing this?"

"The blood is responding to you, not me," Cassian said.

"But I can't control it. I don't know blood magic."

"Your father does," Teague said.

Ros glanced at Cassian and asked, "How do you know how all this works? More secrets?"

He smirked. "Blood is your father's specialty, secrets are mine."

"I guess you think that makes you sound mysterious?" Zandor asked, rolling his eyes.

Cassian replied, "I don't think it does; I *know* it does. And our Princess loves a mystery."

"Uh, guys," Rosalinde said, interrupting their banter, "what's happening to the blood?"

It was rising from the wall, reaching toward her finger. She pulled her hand back to keep it from touching her, but Cassian moved her hand forward again and said, "Let it touch you."

"I don't want to," she said.

He wrapped his arm around her waist and said, "I'm right here and I won't let anything hurt you. I promise."

She nodded, swallowed hard, and reached her finger toward the blood. It moved slowly, as if it was searching for something, until it found her finger. As soon as it did, it rushed from the wall, slid up her finger, and rested in the palm of her hand. It was a perfect circle at first, but after a moment it tilted to the side of her hand, looking for all the world like an arrow.

"What the..."

"I knew it," Cassian said, his tone colored with delight. "Your dad is a genius."

"I don't understand," Ros said.

"He left his blood here on purpose, hoping we would find it. As long as the blood is active, your father is alive. As it withers, so does he. We can use it as a way to track him."

"That sounds a little too convenient," Zandor said.

"He's the only Blood Healer around," Teague said. "How could he know we'd be able to use it? Actually, how are we using it?"

"There's more to blood magic than just healing," Cassian said.

"Like what?" Beckett asked.

"I don't know the details, just *more*," Cassian replied, waving a dismissive hand. He was pacing now, muttering to himself. Ros was only able to pick up one phrase, but it was enough: "*He must've known.*"

She said, "You think he was counting on you to find it."

Cassian met her gaze and nodded. "It's the only thing that makes sense."

"In what way does it make sense that he would leave *blood* for a Night mage?" Zandor asked.

It wasn't impossible, and Ros knew it. Her father had considered marrying Cassian's mother. Even if it had been twenty-five years ago, that didn't mean he would've forgotten everything they shared. Perhaps she had told him about her magic, or at least parts of it, and the king was counting on her son to be able to do the same thing.

Cassian could say something to that effect, could try to explain himself to them, but he didn't. He didn't answer Zandor, or even look at him. His eyes locked on Ros. She could practically feel him begging her to trust him, as if that was the only thing that mattered. And maybe, in that moment, it was.

She knew he was keeping another secret. Maybe it was foolish of her to trust him, but she did. He might not be telling her everything about himself, but he hadn't lied to her. Or at least she didn't *think* he had. So whatever secret he was hiding right then, she would help him. She returned his gaze, hoping he could read the trust on her face as she said, "Everyone has a little darkness in them."

Cassian smiled. "Exactly. I can use the trace amounts of darkness in his blood to activate his leftover magic, but it's the familial tie that anchors it. And look: it's pointing in the direction we need to go."

"This is absurd," Zandor said, pressing his palms against his eyelids.

"You don't have to come," Cassian shrugged.

Zandor chuckled. "Ros, you're not seriously going to go off with this guy, this *stranger*, all because he can move a smudge of blood?"

Ros looked from Zandor to Cassian and back. "I am. There's no reason not to trust him."

"He's from Night house!"

"And you're from Earth," she said. "We all have ties to different places, but that isn't all that defines us. If he can help me find my father, that's all that matters."

Zandor's mouth parted like he was going to argue with her, but she pushed past him and headed down the hall toward the castle proper. Larkin stuck her head out from Elaina's doorway and asked, "What's going on?"

"We're going to find my father," Ros said as she passed. She called to her guard, "We're leaving, Romenia."

She heard Zandor mutter something to his sister, but she didn't stop. She wouldn't stop for him or anyone else, not if she could save her father.

She was nearing her mother's war room before she realized Teague and Beckett weren't with them. It was better that way, she knew. With her father missing, there was a gap in the service the medics could provide. They would need Teague more than ever. Knowing what she did about their relationship, she was willing to bet Beckett wouldn't part from his side, even if he couldn't do much to help the patients.

Ros entered the room with Cassian, Larkin, Zandor, and Romenia. She looked for her mother, but she didn't see her. Instead, she crossed the floor to her sister who had taken up a spot by one of the maps.

"Elsa, I have news," Ros blurted.

"So do I."

"Where's Mother?"

Elsa pursed her lips. "She's trying to fix the mess you made with the Elementalists. That blowhard from Air house has them all riled up. And why were some of them wet?"

Ros winced. In her excitement about going after her father, she'd all but forgotten what happened earlier. "I might've loosed a little magic in the great hall."

"Of course you did," Elsa said, shaking her head.

"It doesn't matter now," Ros said, trying to push past her sister's frustration. "We have a way to track him."

Elsa narrowed her eyes. "What are you talking about?"

Ros explained everything to her sister, whose face remained closed off the whole time. After Rosalinde finished, Elsa asked, "Are you out of your mind?"

"Thank you," Zandor said.

Both Elsa and Ros shot him a "shut your mouth or leave" look, and he pressed his lips into a thin line.

Ros opened her mouth to protest, but Elsa sliced her hand through the air and cut her off. "You're first in line for the throne. You know how this works, Ros, and what happens if we don't find the king soon. If the throne stays empty for more than a week, the other house lords can challenge the law of succession and take control of the kingdom. So time is already ticking down for you to be crowned Queen of Talabrih. You can't go traipsing about the countryside because of a spot of blood that some Dark Elementalist can control."

"He's not controlling it, Elsa. That's not what this is."

"How do you know that?" she asked. "You don't *know* him. Not really."

Cassian took a step forward, but a hand shot forward and grabbed his shoulder as a familiar voice said, "I wouldn't do that, if I were you. The Princess is a tiny thing, but she's fierce."

Elsa laughed as Alaric stepped around the mages and stood between the sisters. Elsa motioned to Alaric and said, "Remember when I said I had news? This was it."

Ros met Alaric's gaze, and as fast as the spark in her chest ignited, she doused it. She could not love him. Instead, she gritted her teeth and said, "I told you not to return."

Alaric's smile faded at her words. His lip curled in a snarl and he said, "Don't worry, *Your Highness*, I'm not here for you."

"Then why are you here?"

He looked to Elsa, refusing to answer Ros directly. "Because I may be the last person who saw the king."

"What? When?" Ros asked.

"Around mid-morning, I'd guess. I was finishing a sword for a customer. He walked through my forge."

Ros furrowed her brows. "Why?"

"No idea," Alaric said. "I tried to talk to him, but it

was like he couldn't hear me. He kept running into things, like he didn't have control of his own body."

"What happened to him?"

"I steered him out. I was afraid he'd get hurt if I left him inside while I went to get help. He wasn't moving very fast, so I went to grab a guard and figured we'd catch up to him, but it took me forever to find someone and when we got back, he was gone."

"You didn't think to come get me?" Ros asked.

His eyes darted to her briefly, then away. Alaric clenched his jaw for a second before saying, "You told me to stay away. So I did."

Ros pressed her hands against her cheeks. "This is an entirely different situation. Of course I would want to know what happened."

"How am I supposed to know what you do and don't want? I'm clearly not very good at reading you, Princess," he said, practically spitting the title at her. "Look, I tried to help. I told a guard. And this evening when I heard he was still missing, I showed up here to tell you what I knew, even after what happened between us. If you want something more than that, ask one of your suitors for it, because I'm done here."

He pushed past Ros and headed for the door. She called after him, but he didn't turn as he stormed out. Ros wanted to go after him, wanted to tell him she was sorry—for this and everything else—but she couldn't. As much as what had happened between them hurt her, she couldn't take a step toward him knowing she would end up pushing him away again.

Instead she focused on what she could do. Despite Elsa's protests, she knew she had to follow the blood signal. She would wait for the others to go to bed and sneak out of the castle. It wasn't a perfect plan, maybe not even a good one, but it was all she had. One way or another, Ros was going to bring her father home.

Eleven

Rosalinde donned her sturdiest boots and warmest cloak. Though the days were warm, she had no idea how long it might take to find her father or where she might stay during the cooler nights. But it didn't matter. She could suffer a little discomfort if it meant saving the king.

She grabbed a bag from her closet that she'd use for food. One stop in the kitchen and she'd be on her way. Ros peeked into the hallway and found it deserted. This time of night, there'd hardly be anyone awake in the castle aside from a handful of guards. Even those who had been working with her mother in the war room would have found rest by now.

She walked down the hall on swift, silent feet. Ros had gotten good at sneaking around the castle through her teenage years. At least now that skill was coming in handy. She made it to the kitchen with minimal issue, forced into hiding only once.

Grabbing a small rind of cheese, a fistful of dried meat, two apples, and some bread leftover from dinner, Ros filled her bag and prepared to leave. She spotted a metal cup beside a small knife on the counter and grabbed them both. As a mage of Water house, she could provide water for herself whenever she needed it, but a cup always made things more convenient. And the knife, well, you could never be too careful.

"Going somewhere?"

Ros winced at her mother's voice. She turned to face her, defeat already plain on her face. She put her pack on the table and said, "I suppose not. How did you know I would try to leave?"

Queen Sariyah gave her an apologetic smile. "Elsabet told me about the blood, and about how she dismissed your idea on how best to use it."

"Dismissing my opinion is a common theme in this family."

"Not intentionally," Sariyah said. "But you are your father's daughter. Eager to do what is right, but too often failing to see the cost of your actions."

"I'm not in the mood for a lecture, mother. I'll return to bed, if it pleases you."

"It does not," Sariyah said. When Ros met her gaze, Sariayh asked, "Do you still have the blood sign?"

Ros held her hand forward. The small spot was still there, shifting with her movements to keep pointing in the direction of her father. She moved her hand around, showing her mother how it worked. Though she didn't explain and Sariyah didn't ask, Rosalinde could almost see the gears moving in her mother's mind. It was one of the rare occasions her mother kept her face unguarded.

"It's amazing," her mother breathed. "And it was the Night mage who gave it life?"

Ros shook her head. "Not exactly. He found it on the wall and tried to use it, but it didn't respond until I got close to it."

Sariyah chewed the inside of her cheek—a habit Ros had picked up from her—before asking, "Is there a chance he's playing you?"

"No," Ros answered, a little too fast.

Her mother smiled. "I don't want to discount anything that may be happening between you, but I'm worried you're growing too attached, too fast."

"I'm trying not to," Ros admitted. "But there's something that keeps drawing me to him."

"He's handsome."

Ros rolled her eyes. "There are plenty of them who are handsome."

"Is he kind?"

"Sometimes," Ros said, as honest as she could be without addressing the darkness she'd seen.

"As kind as Alaric?" When Ros's brows rose, Sariyah said, "I'm not completely oblivious, darling. No one needs as many swords as you commissioned from the blacksmith."

Ros laughed. "It was rather obvious, now that you say it aloud."

"Alaric is a good man. He may be magicless, but I have no doubt he would spend his days making sure you were happy."

"I can't marry a magicless man."

"No," Sariyah said, "you cannot. But you can still keep him. Marry someone you don't love, but who will serve the kingdom. Marry a man who will respect you, who will actively work to support you on the throne, but who will keep a separate bedroom."

Ros knew there was wisdom—and experience—in her mother's words. She could choose someone like Beckett or Teague, someone who wouldn't necessarily love her, but would act with honor and kindness as the King of Talabrih. And she could return to Alaric's arms each night.

Part of her wanted that. But it wasn't fair to either of them, and she knew it. Living that way was only a half-life. Maybe it was too much to think she could find love with one of the Elementalists, but at least she could step aside and let Alaric move on and find it for himself.

Ros shook away thoughts of Alaric and tried to steer her mother back to the situation at hand. "The Night mage may be mysterious, but he has been genuinely helpful to me since he arrived. I don't know if I can fully trust him, but I want to try."

Sariyah sighed. "I truly hope this man is all you think he is, for your sake and your father's."

"Father's?"

Sariyah nodded. "You're going to use the blood to track him."

"Are you serious? You're letting me go?"

"Not alone in the middle of the night, but yes. You can leave after breakfast. We'll have to figure out what to do about the Great Match though. The houses are not going to be happy, but I'm sure we can come up with something to appease them."

Ros wrapped her arms over her mother's shoulders, careful not to smear the blood on her hand, though Cassian had said it would stay put. "Thank you."

"It's not like I could stop you anyway," Sariyah said into her hair. "You go now while you're a princess, or you go in a week when you're a queen. Either way, you'd still go. You're too stubborn for your own good."

"Headstrong," Ros said. "That's the word father uses when he wants it to sound nicer."

Sariyah rolled her eyes. "You're both outrageously *headstrong*. Now, head upstairs and get some rest. You're going to need it."

ROSALINDE WAS at her mother's bedroom door at dawn, but the queen wasn't there.

Ros went to the war room, her father's room. The map tables were empty of their papers, the room empty of guards and strategists, and half-drunk wine sat in glasses beside scraps of food from the night before.

Sariyah was there.

The queen was asleep, curled up in King Tancred's bed, her arms cradling his pillow. Ros had never seen her mother look so vulnerable, or so sad.

Ros moved to the edge of the bed and sat beside her mother. She pushed stray strands of dark hair from her mother's face, humming a song Sariyah used to sing to her when she was a child. It was a depressing song when she sang the words, but without them the tune was sweet, though a bit melancholy.

"I always hated that song," Sariyah whispered. Ros immediately stopped humming, but her mother said, "No, please don't stop."

They sat that way for several minutes, Ros stroking her mother's hair while she hummed a hated song. When the queen finally opened her eyes, they were red-rimmed and tired, but Ros could still see hope there.

"I'm going to find him," she whispered, forcing conviction into her voice.

"I know you will," her mother said.

Sariyah rose and dressed, then called a servant to bring them coffee and sweet rolls. They would still have to take a formal meal in the hall with the Elementalists, but for now, their simple fare was perfect.

"Have you given any thought to what to do about the other houses?" she asked as her mother added fresh cream to her steaming cup.

"I have," Sariyah said. "But I'm still not sure it's going to be enough."

She sipped her coffee while Ros waited for an explanation. When it didn't come right away, Ros said, "Are you going to tell me or should I start guessing?"

"Sorry, I'm a little off right now."

"It's fine, Mother."

Sariyah nodded and put down her cup. "Given the circumstances, we are perfectly within reason to cancel the Great Match altogether. Water and Earth would back that decision, but Air would throw a fit and Fire may be persuaded to side with them. Night, I'm presuming, would side with your decision, but we cannot know that with certainty."

"Or we shorten the Match and I pick someone today."

"That won't work, either. Even with the scores from yesterday's opening ceremony and the opinions of the impartial judges, the house rulers will say you didn't take enough time to get to know their candidates. Most likely, a scandal would ensue, with accusations of impropriety."

Ros huffed. "Why is everything so complicated?"

"Because that's how politics work," Elsa said as she stepped into the room.

"Elsa dear, I didn't hear you come in," Sariyah said.

Elsa shrugged. "I'm sneaky. Sneakier than Ros, at least. I bet I would've made it out last night."

"You know about that too?" Ros asked.

"I've already told you, sis, I'm a good spy. Which is precisely why I'm here."

"What do you mean?" Sariyah asked.

"I've been watching the house rulers and I think I have a plan. Every ruler has a favorite, whether they'll admit it or not, and those favorites match pretty well with yesterday's scorecards."

"They announced the judges' scores?" Ros asked.

Elsa shook her head. "No, but I still know what the scores are."

"How?"

"Better not to ask. Impropriety and all," Elsa said. "Anyway, the rulers and the judges favor Florian from Fire, Zandor from Earth, Teague from Water, and Graeme from Air. No real surprises with those choices. If Ros chooses to narrow down the contenders to that list and has them accompany her on a heroic journey to save the king, they'll gain honor for their bravery *and* we can say she's going to use this time to figure out who she'll marry."

There was silence for a moment while Sariyah and Ros thought over Elsa's plan. After a moment, Sariyah said, "That could actually work."

"It will definitely work. They may balk at first, but they'll see reason when we hold firm. All we have to do is keep our cool." Elsa gave Ros a wry smile and said, "Maybe don't release a tsunami on them."

Ros felt heat rise up her neck. "It's not like I did that

on purpose. And it wasn't even a full tsunami, just a little splash."

Elsa opened her mouth to retort, but Sariyah waved her to be quiet. She turned to Ros and asked, "Is there anyone on the list that you simply can't stand? Or someone you would prefer over those men? A different suitor who may have caught your eye?"

Rosalinde's thoughts immediately turned to Cassian, but she dare not admit it to her mother and sister. At least, not yet, even if they already suspected something. They mistrusted him because of his house affiliation and she didn't want to give them further cause to worry.

"I'm not excited about Florian."

"No one is," Elsa said. "None of the Fire mages impressed anyone yesterday, it seems."

"The Fire Suppressant has an interesting gift."

"They see him as weak," Elsa said.

"He can neutralize their powers in an instant."

"But then what? He doesn't have a way to return fire."

Ros huffed. "I liked him."

"Enough to marry him?" Sariyah asked. "That's the real question here. Did he impress you enough to be a contender for the throne?"

Ros chewed at the inside of her cheek for a second before admitting, "No, not enough."

"What about Orion Bain?" Sariyah asked.

"The crowd loved him," Elsa said. "Judges too."

"And you were always close growing up."

Ros shook her head. "I wouldn't choose him if he were the last Elementalist in Talabrih."

Sariyah and Elsa shared a look, but neither said anything for a moment. Finally, Elsa said, "Then it's Florian. He's the Fire Ruler's son, so their house will be likely to back you if he takes the lead. And honestly, he might be annoying and almost completely useless, but at least he's pretty."

Ros said, "The Combustion mage might be better in a fight."

"Maybe, but Lord le Fevre has been feuding with his father for the past few months. If we want Fire house to go along with this, and we do, Florian is the way to go."

Ros sighed. "Then I guess that list will suffice."

Sariyah's lips curled at the edges as she added, "We must include the Night house as well."

"Must we?" Elsa muttered.

"It's only right."

"Wait," Ros said, "we can't include Teague."

Sariyah asked, "Why not? He's the best Water house has to offer."

"We'll need him to run the medical unit while father is away. I'll take William instead."

"You may need a Healer on your journey. You could get hurt, or the king may need it when you find him," her mother said.

"If we need a Healer, Cassian can return to the castle for Teague," Ros said.

"Right," Elsa said, her lips puckered in distaste. "I

heard about his gift. Interesting, sure. Convenient, definitely. But can you trust him to do the right thing when you need it most?"

"He's given me no reason not to trust him. At every turn, he's been there to help me. I think he's on our side in this."

"I hope so," Sariyah said. "Because I think you're going to need him."

Elsa frowned, but gave a curt nod. "I don't need to trust him. I trust *you*, and if you say he's on our side, then I'll trust in your judgment. Even though I really don't want to."

It wasn't an ideal situation no matter how you looked at it, but Ros was grateful she'd been able to somewhat convince them of Cassian's trustworthiness. Now she just had to hope she was right about him.

Twelve

The women finished making their plans, though they were still shaky at best, before heading to the great hall for breakfast with the nobles attending the Great Match. Sariyah stopped them outside the doors to compose themselves; all three of the royal women had spent most of the night awake and had been up early preparing for how to handle the day. They combed their fingers through tangled hair and smoothed creases from their gowns, all while listening to the chatter in the room beyond.

Rosalinde had a bit less decorum than her mother, peeking around the door to see what was going on. Every table was full of Elementalists; the competitors sat with their entourages, shared conversations with the other house nobles, or begged drinks from passing servants. The room was loud and boisterous, none seeming concerned about their missing king.

Upon the queen's signal, the herald announced the arrival of Sariyah and her daughters. Voices stopped mid-sentence as the assembly rose for their entrance. Chairs and benches scraped against the stone, but all other sounds ceased while the women took their places.

Sariyah sat down, followed by the Princesses, then the remaining guests. Ros was glad to see there was still order amongst the assembly despite all that had happened the evening before. It gave her hope that their plan might succeed.

At the side of the room, the Great Match judges stood waiting to deliver the results from the previous day. Though the women had planned to go right into the scenario they had concocted, Ros sensed the judges words might lend some credit to the decisions they'd already made. She waved them forward to give the results.

The whole room seemed to lean in closer, as if it would help them hear better. One of the judges stepped forward. He was an older man, late sixties perhaps, with thick white hair brushed back from a large forehead overrun by bushy eyebrows. He wore a silver armband denoting he was a member of Air house. "Esteemed guests, it is my honor to present the scores of our exceptional Air competitors this year:

Brensen Cavoll, five;

Yaro Surrick, five;

Merritt Mahone, six;

Jericho Tevachaly, seven;

Graeme Monsanato, ten."

A stern-looking woman with a green armband stepped forward as the Air judge moved back in line. Despite her rigid appearance, her voice was sweet as she said, "I am pleased to announce the scores of Earth house:

Keaton Page, two;

Rylen Fielder, three;

Evran Allen, five;

Galagorn Wentwell, five;

Hesh Svenson, six;

Beckett Chastain, seven;

Lyzandor Zolto, nine."

Rosalinde smiled to herself. Things were going just as her sister had predicted. Though she wasn't sure how Elsa had gotten the results, she supposed it didn't really matter. All that mattered was getting through breakfast so they could leave to find her father.

She looked down at the blood still sitting on her hand, still guiding her path. It was the only lead she had and she was terrified something would go wrong. She'd been very careful not to wipe her hand against anything or even wash it when she had hastily cleansed the rest of her body before getting dressed that morning. If something happened to that single drop of blood, she would lose any chance she had of bringing her father back.

Ros looked up as she felt someone watching her. Her gaze immediately found Cassian's. From the other end of the table, he pointed to the palm of his own hand as if to ask about the blood on hers. She nodded and gave him a smile. She was pleased to see the relief on his face, as if his expression confirmed the things she had told her family about him. There was undoubtedly more to unravel about the Night house mage, but at least she was certain he was on her side.

As the nonbinary judge finished giving the scores of Fire house, Ros realized she hadn't been paying attention. One glance at Florian's dour expression was all the confirmation she needed that he had not done as well as he wished. If Elsa's predictions were correct, he still led the other Fire competitors, or at least most of them, though not by much. The other nobles slapping his back showed him to be the favorite of his house, as Elsa had stated.

The Water house judge was a friend of Rosalinde's mother, a well-to-do merchant named Marina van Howson. She was always impeccably dressed, today being no exception. Marina wowed in a stunning outfit of silk in various shades of blue that made her eyes as bright as a summer sky. She announced Teague in the lead, as expected, with a ten. William, Phineer, and Nico were right behind him with two nines and an eight, respectively.

"Because we have no Night house judge," Marina continued, "I will give the score of our rarest competitor: Cassian Scalise, eight."

Eight, Ros thought. She had given him a one, and he still managed one of the highest scores. Had she scored him appropriately rather than out of fear and hurt, he would've equaled Graeme and Teague.

As soon as Marina stepped aside, Queen Sariyah stood. "Thank you, dear friends and judges, for delivering the verdicts for yesterday's opening ceremony. It seems as if this year's competition is one of talented mages indeed." She raised her glass and said, "A toast to all our fine participants: may you be forever blessed by your gifts, your houses, and the elements."

"The elements," the crowd echoed, raising glasses of their own.

As they tipped back their glasses and sat back down, Queen Sariyah said, "Though I'm grateful for the gifted Elementalists competing for my daughter's hand, this year's Great Match will not be the standard format you're used to. As you all know, our beloved king is missing. Naturally, this changes how we proceed."

Hessian Barclay was on his feet before she'd finished speaking. "You can't change the format of the Match at your whim. With King Tancred missing, decisions should fall to the house rulers."

Ros stood next to her mother, lifting her head in defiance of Hessian's words. "That's presumptuous of you, Lord Barclay, considering *I'm* the heir to the Talabrih throne. If anyone is going to decide my fate, it will be me."

"I did not mean offense," he clipped out. "But your judgment may be clouded in this area. You would not be the first young person to be swayed by a pretty face or a *mysterious*"—he shot a look at Cassian—"stranger."

"I assure you, I am impressed with but unmoved by the contestants thus far. My heart is with my father, not the competition."

Hessian smirked. "A perfect example of why we should continue with the rulers assisting you."

Elsa cleared her throat, reminding Ros to keep her cool. Rosalinde was thankful her sister and mother were able to handle their emotions so easily, but something about Hessian Barclay set her teeth on edge.

Ros clenched her fists at her side while forcing a smile. "Not to worry, noble Elementalists. Today I leave to find my father, and with his return, I will be able to give myself fully to the process."

"You expect us to wait around while you go on a wild quest? That's hardly reasonable."

"Of course not," Sariyah said. "That would never do. Instead, Princess Rosalinde will select a hero from each house to accompany her and she will choose her husband from among them."

Barclay scoffed, but Ros spoke before he could object. "Thanks to the judges' announcements, the selection has already been made. I will take the mages with the highest score from each house, as long as they are willing to accompany me."

There was a grumble throughout the room as twenty hopefuls and those accompanying them realized they were being dismissed without receiving the full week to impress. Before they could grow too upset, Queen Sariyah said, "I understand this is a disappointment for some of you. Though the rest of you will not get a chance to marry my daughter, we would like to offer you an alternative arrangement to make up for the change."

Elsabet stood and said, "There are multiple nobles of marrying age throughout the kingdom. We will invite them to the castle for three days, to hold a miniature Match for you, allowing you to find the best prospect from among them. In addition, the crown will provide an extra dowry for whomever you choose, essentially making each person equal to the next, giving you the opportunity to choose based on the quality of your connection with the individual."

There was silence in the room for a moment, but it quickly erupted as the nobles began talking to one another about the proposition. The women had expected this, counted on it even; it was the next part that would determine the course for everything else.

While the other houses argued, Cassian Scalise sauntered forward from his place at the table and bowed low. The other Elementalists quieted to hear him say, "Your proposal is fair and prudent. Though I am the lone representative of Night house, I would offer myself to be at your disposal even without the sensibility of this new arrangement. Command me as you see fit."

"Thank you, Lord Scalise, for your kindness. We are grateful for the assistance and look forward to forging a strong relationship with Night house," the queen said.

There was a pause after he spoke, but it was soon followed by Florian from Fire house stepping forward from their seats and bowing to Sariyah, Ros, and Elsa. Rosalinde's gaze flicked to the Fire house ruler and Florian's father, Gilthroy le Fevre. His long fair hair was pulled back from his rugged face—sharp angles that Florian inherited—while his seafoam eyes focused on his son. His look made it clear he was relying on his son to deliver the message for his house, whatever it may be.

Florian gave a broad, charming smile as he looked between the women. "The Elementalists of Fire house accept your proposal and will do everything we can to help find King Tancred. Because the Fire lords had several competitors equally ranked, Lord le Fevre has chosen me, as his heir, to represent Fire house. We are at your service."

Sariyah matched his expression, saying, "Great friends, we thank you for your understanding and acceptance. Are all of the Fire house competitors mollified by this decision?"

Ros watched the nodding heads of the Fire house mages. Whether they were happy with this turn of events or not, none were willing to speak against their house lord.

"Aye, My Queen," Lord le Fevre said. "Our house serves the throne."

Sariyah nodded. "We are in your debt, my lord."

Even as she spoke, the ruler of Earth house stepped forward with her competitors in tow. Lady Valeria

Auguste was a young woman only a few years older than Ros. In fact, Ros still remembered watching Valeria's Great Match five or six years ago when she chose a soft-spoken Water house woman who could conjure rain from a clear sky. Despite Valeria's youthfulness, she was a formidable woman, eager to battle with words, wise in the ways youth seldom are. She had a strong aptitude for ruling, returning her house to a prosperity it hadn't known for generations.

"Earth house accepts your wisdom in this situation, Queen Sariyah. We place our trust in Princess Rosalinde to find the match that will best serve her life on the throne, as well as the lives of her people. Command us as you see fit."

Nico, Teague, Phineer, and William came forward. For a moment, Ros wondered why they stood but did not speak. Then she realized with her father gone, *she* was the ruler of Water house. She stepped forward to them and said, "Though I am ruler of your house, I will not command you to agree to these terms. The choice must be yours."

Teague nodded and said, "With respect, Your Highness, I must decline the opportunity to accompany you. My place is here, in the medical unit."

"I understand and wish you well," Ros said. "I relinquish any claim to your heart or your hand and free you of the bond of the Great Match. Return to your patients with my blessing."

William lifted his chin and said, "As the second

highest score of Water house, it would be my honor to join you."

"You were tied," Ros said, turning toward Phineer. "What is your wish, Wavemaker Gohn?"

He took a deep breath and let it out slowly. "I came to the Great Match in the hopes of introducing you to the work I do, so that we might have a partnership in helping others. However, in my heart of hearts, I have never desired to be a king."

"Which is the very reason you'd make a good one," Ros said.

Phineer smiled. "Perhaps that is the way of things. Those who desire power should never have it."

"You are wise, good sir, and though you do not wish to continue in this, I do hope we can develop a working relationship in the future. I believe in what you're doing, and I would like to help advance your cause."

"That is a blessing," Phineer said. "I wish you a safe journey, Princess, and I truly hope you find your father."

Ros turned to Nicolai and asked, "Lord Bardeaux, will you agree to the arrangement my sister proposed?"

He nodded. "As it pleases you, Your Highness."

Turning back to William, she said, "I accept your offer, good sir."

"I live to serve, Princess."

Ros looked out to Hessian Barclay. He was still in a heated discussion with the mages of Air house, seeming to have missed the other houses pledging their acceptance of the changes to the Great Match. Rosalinde said, "Air house, have you made a decision?"

Graeme Monsanato pulled his arm out of Barclay's grip and stormed forward. He dropped to his knee and said, "My Lady, I will do everything in my power to assist in finding my king. Though the rest of my house may be in turmoil, my heart is decidedly yours."

Ros blinked, surprised by his declaration. The other house rulers seemed to be fine with the changes, but the scowl on Hessian's face made it clear he was not. Elsa had said Barclay would agree since they were choosing the house favorites, but it seemed he had placed his favor on someone other than Graeme. Ros wasn't sure which mage he wanted to win, but it didn't matter now. The remaining Air Elementalists, Jericho, Yaro, Brensen, and Merritt, made their way forward and gave their agreement to abide by the plan.

With Sariyah and Elsa set to iron out the details of the miniature Match with the house lords, Rosalinde was now ready to search for King Tancred. She looked down at the tiny drop of blood in her hand, knowing it would lead her where she wanted to go. She turned in the direction the blood was pointing, and when she looked up, she wasn't surprised to see Cassian smiling back.

Thirteen

The sun had long faded behind the distant mountains when Ros finally agreed to stop. She would have continued until she was exhausted, physically incapable of going farther, if Cassian hadn't been there to convince her of the futility of it. It was too dark to see where they were going and too dangerous to keep pressing on. Besides, she could barely make out the blood on her hand as the darkness clung to her like a wet shirt dripping midnight.

They'd been riding since midday. There had been very little fanfare as they left the castle, just a few rushed goodbyes and well wishes. Some of the nobles had stood outside to wish them well, but most seemed to have given up any interest they'd had in Rosalinde as soon as it was decided they were no longer contenders for the throne. Few of the townsfolk knew of their journey and they left early enough to avoid prying eyes, but Ros had noticed a certain blacksmith lurking outside his forge as they passed. When Ros and Alaric's eyes met, she tried to give him a reassuring smile, but he turned and walked away. She wasn't sure why it mattered to her, or what he wanted from their exchange, but there was a distinct part of her heart that felt bruised when she thought of what had transpired between them.

So, she wouldn't think of him. Alaric could not be part of her future, and her present was dedicated to saving her father.

The servants had packed bags of food for them as well as some warm clothes and traveling provisions. The queen had assigned guards to go with them, but Rosalinde had dismissed them summarily, knowing they would do nothing but slow her down. It took a bit of convincing, but with Rosalinde's reminder that she would soon be queen and able to decide if they remained on staff or not, eventually all but Romenia departed. Romenia wouldn't leave no matter what Ros said, insisting that she would do her part to protect the royal family no matter what her commands were. Eventually Rosalinde gave in and let her come along.

Graeme had wanted to use his wind phoenix to travel, and Ros had been eager to agree to the speed, but the Air mage wasn't sure he could carry everyone. There was also a concern that she would lose access to her blood token, as they weren't sure exactly how it worked. Cassian had said it was spelled to remain on her hand as long as her father was alive, but Rosalinde was still careful to keep it protected.

Rosalinde rode atop the piebald, Mercutio, while Cassian took the moody Palomino, Desdemona. Ros didn't know the names of the others, but she had watched with interest as each seemed to choose their rider rather than the other way around. Florian found himself on the blood bay, looking for all the world like a terrified little boy who'd never seen a horse up close. William rode the dapple gray, smoothing her hair and whispering kind words of encouragement as they plodded along. Zandor was at ease on the white, a natural in the saddle, while Graeme took the midnight black beauty who seemed as wary of him as he was of her. Romenia trailed behind them on a horse of her own, though she somehow managed to make the beast look small.

Ros looked down at her hand one last time, trying to make out the dark spot on her palm. No matter how much she wanted to continue, she knew stopping was the right decision.

"Don't worry, Princess. We'll start fresh in the morning," Cassian said. He reached up to help her down from Mercutio.

"I know," she sighed as she climbed down. "I just don't want to waste any time. He could be hurt or in danger."

"So could we, if we don't stop. We can't risk taking the horses over ground we can't see."

She nodded, but her heart ached at the thought of her father out there somewhere, unable to save himself from whoever or whatever had done this.

"I'll get a fire going," Florian said, pulling Ros from her thoughts.

"No, wait," Cassian said.

But it was too late. He grabbed the reins of the closest horses as a bolt of lightning shot from Florian's hand. The fire caught, giving them enough light to see Florian and Graeme's horses running toward the tree line in a tizzy. Cassian cursed, then growled, "I guess I'll grab Minola and Lady Macbeth."

"I'll go," Romenia offered.

"I can help too. I'm good with animals," Zandor said.

Cassian's eyes narrowed for a moment, but the expression was gone before it had a chance to take shape. With a nod, the three went in search of the frightened creatures.

Ros watched the interaction, unsure what to expect. The obvious disdain Zandor had for Cassian was frustrating and misplaced, but Ros knew talking to him about it wouldn't help. Zandor was worried about her, didn't trust Cassian, and though she didn't want to admit it, she was certain he was a bit jealous. She hoped it would change while they were out on their quest and he was able to get to know Cassian better, but until it did, there wasn't much she could do about it.

"Hungry, Princess? I can get some food started,"

William said. He gave Ros a smile. "I'm a surprisingly good cook, you know."

"That's wonderful news, because I'm rubbish," Ros said.

Florian asked, "Have you actually tried?"

"Of course. I'll have you know I've tried nearly every job in the castle at one time or another because I wanted to know what life is like for the people doing them."

"Whoa now," Florian said, throwing up his hands, "no judgment here. I've personally never set foot inside a kitchen and I have no plans to. I'd likely just burn the place down."

"At least I tried," Ros muttered.

William said, "Maybe you just haven't had the right teacher. When we get back to the castle, I'd be happy to give you some lessons."

"Why wait, chef? Give us all a lesson now," Florian said, smirking.

William's cheeks went red. "Not a lot to work with out here. What I'm making is enough to hold body and soul together, but that's about it."

"I'm certain I wouldn't retain it even if you tried," she said. "Now that we've stopped riding, I can barely keep my eyes open."

"You should rest, Princess," William said. "We'll take care of everything."

She looked between the three mages unpacking near the fire, wondering what these men were thinking and whether or not they wished they were somewhere else.

Their words had been genuine back in the great hall, she was sure, but offering help became something different when it meant sleeping on the hard ground. It was only the first night, but still, they were here and she was grateful.

"You can call me Ros," she said, directing her words to the three of them. "No need for titles or formalities out here."

William smiled up from the food he was organizing. "Pleasure to know you, Ros. I'm Will."

"I'm still Florian," the Fire mage said. Though he smiled with the words, Ros was sure she heard a little snark in his tone.

"Ah yes, the same fool as always, no matter what you call him," Graeme said, the same forced smile and snarky tone Florian had used.

"Are we going to do this now, in front of the Princess?" Florian asked.

"I'm sure Lady Ros is as repulsed by your attitude as the rest of us. We're here to find our king, her beloved father, not to play at being nobles or act like we're too good to be out here."

Florian sighed. "I said my name, Graeme, nothing more."

"You've made your snide comments all afternoon, from complaints about your horse—"

"That horse is out to get me," Florian interrupted.

"—to the weather—"

"I did not pack the right clothes for this excursion."

"—to the direction of the wind."

"I mean, shouldn't you be able to help with that?"

Graeme threw his hands up and huffed. "We haven't been away from our creature comforts for a full day and you're already unbearable."

"It's not like you're a delight to be around either," Florian said.

"At least I'm here, trying to do what's right for Princess Rosalinde."

"You are so predictable," Florian said, rolling his eyes. "If you really want to drag her into this, why not tell Ros what you're really mad about."

Will tried to cut in, saying, "Maybe we should all calm down—"

"Stay out of this, Will. Graeme has something to tell our princess," Florian said.

Ros folded her arms across her chest. "This needs to stop. Now. I don't need to hear whatever sordid thing happened between the two of you."

Florian smirked. "Isn't this your time to get to know us so you can make an informed decision? Because really, this is something you *should* know."

Without a word, Graeme stormed away from the fire.

Ros glared daggers at Florian, saying, "Whatever your problem is, you need to drop it. Pick it back up when we return to the castle if you must, but out here, we are all we have. We need to be able to rely on one another."

"How should I do that, *Ros*? It's impossible to rely on someone you can't trust, and I wouldn't count on

Graeme to spit on me if I were on fire. He's more likely to fan the flames."

"He's not the only one here," Ros said.

"Ah, yes, there's also the completely trustworthy and not at all shady Night house mage who appeared out of nowhere hours before the king went missing. Some of us see through his charm."

"You're being disrespectful," William said, balling his fists at his side.

"I'm being honest," Florian said. "I doubt many people respect her enough to do that with her. Maybe it would do her good to listen."

"All you've done so far is show you don't want to be here," Ros said.

"Fair point," Florian said.

"Then why did you volunteer?" she asked.

"There wasn't much choice. My father told me I was coming along."

Ros huffed. "Surely he could have sent someone else. Were there no true volunteers from Fire house?"

"There was," he said. Florian's eyes studied her face when he said, "Orion Bain wanted to come. I thought that might be a bad idea, considering…"

Will looked between them. "Considering what?"

Ros knew her face had already given everything away to Florian. She couldn't control it. The very mention of that man's name sent rage coursing through her.

"He's had some unsavory things to say about Ros in the past," Florian said. "Based on what I know of him, I was certain his words were lies. Still, if there was even a morsel of truth to them, I thought it best to keep a distance between him and the Princess."

She blew out the breath she was holding as she tried to calm her nerves. The thought that Orion had volunteered to come with her to find the king made her want to punch something. The fact that Florian had saved her from that made it even worse.

"I appreciate that," she said. "We have an unpleasant history and I'd prefer not to be too close with Orion Bain."

A silence passed between them for several minutes. When Will went back to preparing food, Florian leaned closer and whispered, "I'm sorry for whatever he did to you."

"Are you? Is that why you threw his name at me the way you did?"

"That was cruel of me. I wanted to confirm... No, there's no excusing it."

"Were you telling the truth? Did he really volunteer?"

Florian nodded. "I was afraid of what could happen if he got you alone. When I told my father I didn't want him to send Bain, my fate was sealed. But I'd do it again in a heartbeat. Even with the others here, it didn't feel safe."

"So, other women have complained against him?"

Florian nodded. "Two this year."

"And yet he remains one of the nobles of your house? One of your illustrious competitors, even?"

"It's more complicated than that," Florian said.

"It shouldn't be."

Their eyes met, and Ros could see anger burning in his. "I know. It won't always be this way. When I have power, real power, in my house, people like Orion will pay for their crimes."

"In the meantime, he's free to do what he wants to whomever he wants?"

"Until someone is willing and able to stand up to him, yes."

"How many women do you think he's hurt while people sit idly by?"

"Hard to say. More than have come forward. And just think, if he was willing to do that to you, there's no one he wouldn't hurt."

"Someone saved me from him," she whispered.

"Then you were lucky. When we get back, maybe we should work together and see how many we might be able to save."

Ros nodded. Florian was right—someone had to do something. She'd been so scared to talk about what had happened, to admit what he'd done to her. Even the night it happened when she'd gotten Alaric to the clinic, she didn't tell a soul he'd been hurt protecting her.

But the time for fear was over. Orion Bain, and any like him, needed their titles and their money stripped from them, and justice brought to their doorstep instead. Florian might be arrogant and a bit of a jerk, but there were worse things to be. If he was willing to help her better the kingdom by eliminating the power structure that protected people like Orion, that made him okay in her eyes.

Now all she had to do was convince everyone else of that. Starting with Graeme.

Fourteen

~

She walked into the darkness in the same direction Graeme had gone. Away from the fire, the night took over again. The Air mage was nothing more than a shadow against the black of the terrain, but the darkness did nothing to hide his heavy, ragged breathing.

"I was hoping you'd stay by the fire," Graeme said, his voice so low it took Ros a second to work out his words. "Not that I don't desire your company, but this is no place for the future Queen of Talabrih."

"Nor for a man who could become king," she said.

He laughed, but the sound was bitter. "Not much chance of that with Florian around."

"Whatever secret he has on you doesn't really matter. We all have a past, Graeme."

"Aye, we do. The secret...well, it's not the secret that's the problem. It's the things that happened because of the secret, the things that are *still* happening."

"And what things are those?"

He sighed. "It doesn't matter, Princess. I'd rather not pour my troubles on you when you have enough of your own."

"You're out here with me, sharing my troubles and lightening my load. Maybe I can do the same for you, if you're willing to let me."

Graeme sighed. "Seems a shame to complain about my past, when others have it far worse."

"Don't compare your struggles to others," she said. "Everyone experiences things differently. Just because someone else might have it bad, doesn't diminish the pain you're feeling."

"My pain though, is simply part of a tale as old as time. I was in love."

Ros was glad for the darkness then, so Graeme couldn't read the surprise on her face. Though why she was surprised, she couldn't say. Plenty of people had dalliances prior to their marriages. Several scenarios flitted through her head, but the first question to appear in all of them was, "Do I know her?"

"Probably. She's from a noble Fire house family."

"Which girl?" she asked, though from the interaction with Florian, she could guess.

"I'm not sure I should say," he muttered. "Though I certainly can bring no further dishonor to her now."

Ros whispered, "It was Cordelia le Fevre, wasn't it? Florian's sister."

He nodded. "She was...everything."

"I'm not sure why that's a problem. Many people find love before they're matched. Were the families unhappy? Did she return the feelings?"

"She loved me, too," Graeme said. Ros could hear hurt in his voice as he said the words. Again she was grateful it was dark, but this time it was because she couldn't bear to see his face when the words broke him. "And we, well, we did what people do when they're in love."

"Is that supposed to be the big secret that disqualifies you from the Great Match? Because it's not a big deal."

"She was with child," he said in a rush. "Her family sent her away. I was furious, searched everywhere for her, but they'd hidden her well. Florian was my best friend, like my brother. I thought he would help me. Instead, he turned me away, all because I'd dared to love his sister."

"What happened to her?"

"She returned after having our baby. But the child wasn't with her. She abandoned him to someone else to raise."

"I'm sorry," Ros whispered. She knew the words weren't enough, but she didn't know what else to say.

"I tried to find out where our child was, but she wouldn't tell me. We got in a huge fight about it and I said things I didn't mean. I returned for her the next day, thinking we could work it out but..."

He let the words trail off and Ros was afraid to ask more. She had heard rumors that Cordelia had disappeared and now she knew why. Graeme's secret was that he had fallen in love, disgraced the Fire house's first daughter, and because of him she was gone, probably never to return. It was a scandal, but it wasn't as if he'd done something out of malice.

After a moment of quiet, Ros asked, "Do you still love her?"

"Yes," he whispered without even a pause.

"Well, that could put a damper on our relationship."

"I don't want you to get hurt, Princess, but I'm not here for a love match. I want to be king, I *need* to be king, to try to fix this system and make sure no one else loses the love of their life like I did."

His words struck Ros to her core. She wasn't worried that he wasn't interested in her—she knew love was far less important than finding the right man to be by her side. But listening to him talk about making things better for Talabrih clarified they were on two paths to the same goal. Graeme wasn't here to fall in love with her, but he was here to improve the land she loved.

"Thank you for telling me your secret," she said. "It can't have been easy, especially considering what it could cost you."

He sighed. "I hope you'll at least let me help find your father before you send me away."

"I'm not sending you away."

"What? After all I've told you..."

"You told me of a man in love, a man who wishes to do better for his kingdom. Those are not reasons to disqualify you. If anything, my opinion of you is higher."

"Doesn't the thought of a lost heir frighten you? What if we're married and my child comes looking for his father?"

"If anything, we would search for your child and try to bring them home to you."

"I don't know what to say. This is not the answer I expected. You are not the woman I envisioned would be inheriting the throne."

"I want the best for Talabrih. Having someone at my side who is willing to sacrifice their own happiness for the betterment of our land, well, that's the best I could hope for."

Light crept up behind Ros, shining on Graeme's face as he stood in front of her. For the first time since following him away from the campfire, she could see he was smiling. It wasn't the boisterous thing that Florian wore, or Cassian's smirk, but something entirely different. Graeme's smile looked shy, like he was afraid to show it.

"Ros, are you alright?"

She turned toward the light behind them where Cassian stood with a torch. "We're fine. Just having a chat."

The light shone in her eyes and she couldn't see Cassian's face, but she could almost hear the concern as he said, "Perhaps you could finish your chat near the camp. It's dangerous to wander off out here."

"He's right," Graeme said. "I should have known better than to step so far from the fire."

"Yes, you should have," Cassian grumbled. He extended his arm for Ros to take it and led her back toward the fire.

As they walked, Ros asked, "Did you get the horses?"

Cassian nodded. "Thanks to Romenia," he said, then hesitatingly, "and Zandor."

"Oh, you two have made up?" she asked.

He chuckled. "I wouldn't go that far. But I'm grateful for his help."

They were within the campfire's light when they heard the first howl. Rosalinde's heart hammered in her chest and she clutched at Cassian's arm. She knew there were beasts along the roads, had heard tales from travelers about wolves and bears and other, darker things that probably weren't real.

"Come on," he said, wrapping his arm around her and pulling her closer to the fire.

A trio of howls erupted into the night, closer than before. Romenia slid her sword from its scabbard, her eyes darting about as the firelight danced upon her blade.

"Wolves?" Florian asked. He lounged by the fire, digging an ornamental dagger into the ground beside him.

"Let's hope so," Cassian said.

"Come now," Florian said. "Tell me you're not one of those who believes the stories about the other things that come out at night. I took you for a practical man, if not a very bright one."

Cassian's jaw clenched. "I believe in what my eyes can

see, little lordling. And trust me, my eyes have seen far more than yours ever will. Including a few things that would make your spoiled skin crawl."

Florian raised his hands. "Calm down, darkling. I only meant—"

"I know what you meant."

Another howl broke into their conversation. Zandor said, "They're coming from the tree line. Can we give them an elemental push to get them to back off? Water or Air, maybe?"

"Don't," Cassian said. His voice was quiet, but commanding. All eyes were on him as he said, "Until we know for sure what's in those trees, we can't risk it."

"What do you think is out there?" Ros asked.

He pressed his lips together and shook his head. "Nothing good."

Before he could say more, an earsplitting screech echoed across the area where they'd made camp. Ros turned toward the sound. It was unlike anything she'd ever heard, far from the howls of the could-be wolves.

Then she saw it. It was too dark to make out its features, but she could see a massive shape swaying in front of the trees. It was bigger than a wolf, bigger than a horse even, but she reminded herself it could still be something natural and not like the monsters from the travelers' stories.

Florian stood beside her now, staring out into the darkness at something they couldn't quite see. Without warning, he flicked his hand and lightning cracked at the tree line beside the beast, lighting it up for one terrible, fear-confirming second.

"No," Florian breathed. "Impossible. Was th-that a..."

Cassian swallowed hard. "Yeah. There's a vuljasari over there and you just pissed her off."

The beast's image was burned into Rosalinde's mind. It was slightly bigger than a bear standing on its back legs, but hairless, with large, exaggerated orb-like eyes the color of a starless sky. Stark white against the tree line when the lightning struck, there were only two hints of color on its body: the thick, bulging veins tinged canary-yellow and the gory mess of red around its mouth. It was a thing of nightmares.

"Vuljasari?" Ros stammered. "I didn't think they were real."

"Oh, they're real, Princess," Cassian said.

Florian said, "Build up the fire. Stick close to it. That'll keep her away."

Cassian shook his head, pulling Ros back behind the others. "Doesn't work."

"Silver and salt?" Zandor asked.

"No," Cassian said. "Get to the horses. Slowly. Move too fast and she'll charge."

"The horses?" Ros asked.

"We'll have to outrun it."

"Coward," Graeme spat.

Cassian's jaw clenched, but he kept pushing Ros

toward the horses. "Fight if you want. I won't stop you if you have a death wish."

Graeme said, "If we all fight together—"

"Then we all die together," Cassian finished. "This isn't a fairytale. You heard the howls? That was her babies. She's hunting for their dinner."

"We have a chance to rid the world of those things."

"Those *things* have as much right to life as we do. I don't want to get eaten by them, but I won't try to destroy them, either."

"That's cute," Graeme said. "A pacifist Night mage."

"You don't know the first thing about my people," Cassian growled.

"And hopefully I never will. If we're lucky, the other houses will join together and wipe you out before there are any more of you. Just like I'm going to wipe out that vuljasari."

Ros flinched, shocked by the vitriol spewing from Graeme. Only a few minutes ago, she was listening to him talk about being in love and the consequences of that. She was considering how he would be as King of Talabrih and how he would treat his people. Now all she could see was the darkness in his eyes.

Darkness, she thought, her eyes going wide. She could see it now, almost like an aura radiating around him. She could *see* the darkness consuming him, just like it had consumed her in the great hall. Whether it was from dwelling on the past and letting himself succumb to the pain of loss, or if a hatred burned in him for the monsters of the night, she couldn't say. All she knew was that he had transformed in the blink of an eye, and he was no longer the same man she'd been talking to only moments before.

Cassian's words cut into her thoughts. "She will rip you limb from limb."

"Has to catch me first," Graeme said.

He shot up into the air, buoyed by a gust of wind. There was a howl, louder than any of those before, and it sent a chill down Rosalinde's back.

Cassian yelled, "Romenia, to the Princess." He clasped Rosalinde's hand and she felt them move through the night as he teleported them the rest of the way to the horses. He lifted her onto Mercutio and as soon as she had her hands on his reins, he slapped the horse's rear and sent it flying into the night.

There was distant yelling, and she thought she heard another horse galloping behind her, but over the sounds of Mercutio's hoofbeats and the pounding of her own heart, she couldn't be sure.

Ros tried to look back over her shoulder to see what was happening, but Mercutio raced headlong into the darkness and all she could see was the faint spot of campfire as it diminished to a speck behind them, then nothing at all.

Fifteen

Ros lost track of time as the horse careened through the night. Fear raced through her mind, out of control; all she wanted was to make sure the others were okay, but the very sight of the vuljasari had sent such a panic through the group that she was afraid of what might happen if she tried to return. After a while, minutes or hours, she didn't know, Mercutio slowed to a walk. She felt relief push through all her other emotions, knowing the horse had at last stopped sensing danger around them.

She looked around in the darkness, unable to make out anything through the trees. Lost in her thoughts, Ros hadn't noticed when they entered the forest, but now the dark canopy above and the shadowed trunks around them gave her an uneasy feeling.

Ros took a deep breath to steady her nerves. She

loved the woods in the daylight, but now the dangers lurking just out of sight were all she could think about.

She didn't know where she was or how she would find the others again. Out of all the scenarios she'd run through her head as she and Mercutio had careened through the night, one thing was clear: she had to keep going, no matter how much she wanted to go back for her companions. She kept reminding herself that they were powerful Elementalists, that they could defend themselves, and that her father was still out there needing her help. She needed to press down her emotions, figure out where she was, and form a plan for what she would do next—with or without the rest of the group.

"Okay, Mercutio," she said, leaning forward to pat the horse's neck, "let's get out of these woods, eh? You got us to safety, brave boy. Now we'll find a place to wait for the others, somewhere I can make a little pool for you to get a good drink after all your hard work."

Almost as soon as she'd said the words aloud, she heard water nearby. It sounded like a steady stream, and since she knew they hadn't crossed one earlier in the day, she deduced she must've ridden in the opposite direction of the castle when Cassian sent her off. Whether that was good or bad, she didn't know.

The trees thinned out as they approached the water, giving way to a full moon above. The light set the area before her aglow, stained in silver. The thick under-brush had given way to a flower-lined path that seemed to ebb and flow around the horse's feet. She climbed off Mercutio and led him to the water's edge. He sniffed at the stream, but wouldn't drink. Instead, he jerked his head back, trying to pull his reins from her grasp.

She gave up trying to force Mercutio to the stream and instead rummaged through her saddlebag until she found what she was looking for. She'd put a small bowl in her bag so she could wash herself without the need to find water. Thankfully, Cassian hadn't had time to unpack Mercutio with the fiasco of the other horses running away.

She focused her magic as small as she could—a chore for her, to be sure—and after a few minutes of accidentally spraying herself in the face, she managed to slosh a bit of water into the bowl. Mercutio gulped at it greedily and she refilled it several times before he seemed to have his fill.

"Smart horse," a saccharine-sweet voice said.

Ros jumped. Her eyes jerked in the direction of the voice, but no one was there.

"Over here," it said again.

She caught sight of the voice's owner this time, though just barely. It was a flicker at the corner of her vision, something she couldn't quite look at. Ros turned her head to stare at a tree in the distance and let her peripheral vision catch the glimmer of a figure off to her right. Though she couldn't be sure of any details, the speaker was humanoid in appearance and about the size of a child. She saw flashes of silver as it moved, though she couldn't be sure if it was hair or skin or clothes reflecting moonlight.

Moonlight, she thought. *There wasn't moonlight when we were setting up camp because it's a new moon. So why could she see it now?*

"Why are you here, human?" the creature asked.

"I got lost," Ros said. She'd heard stories of creatures like this, sprites and fae and a host of other things. All the tales said they could hear it if you lied, and they didn't like it. Best to keep her answers true and as short as possible.

"Your horse is tired."

"Yes," Ros said.

"I'd hoped to steal him away from you. He's a lovely one. But he refused my water."

"He is a fine horse," she said carefully.

"Will you drink my water, so I may have control of you?"

"No, thank you."

A tinkle of laughter filled the air. "You're a talkative one, aren't you? I could ask you different questions if I wanted, pull the truth from you. But I'm not after you, human, not truly, so I won't force your words if you do not wish to speak them."

Ros was taken aback, unsure how to proceed. The more she interacted with the creature, the more likely she was to be ensnared by it. Then again, she probably wouldn't meet anyone else out here, wherever here was, and perhaps this one could help her get back to the others.

"We were running from a vuljasari. My friends and I were attacked."

The creature made a soft sound, like air sucking through their teeth. "Vuljasari. Terrible things, when they're hungry. But if you're alive, you weren't attacked."

"My friend put me on the horse and sent me running before it made it into camp."

"They aren't here and you are, so they put your safety before their own. Sounds like a good friend."

"Yes," Ros croaked, a sob rising in her throat.

"Oh, don't cry, human. I hate it when you do that."

"Sorry," she said, trying to hold back her tears. "It's just, I don't know if they're alive or...or..."

The tears poured from her eyes, no matter how hard she tried to hold them back. The little creature made a frustrated noise in their throat and said, "Please stop. I can't stand the sounds you're making."

Ros sobbed harder, stammering, "I'm sorry," between hiccups.

"Fine, fine, I'll make you a deal: you stop crying and I'll grant you a wish."

"A wish?" she asked. She still couldn't make out the creature's form, but there weren't many in the old stories who could grant wishes. That, combined with the unnatural moonlight, left her with one conclusion. "You're a Moonchild."

She got the distinct impression it was rolling its eyes at her as it said, "Oy, so clever, aren't you."

There was a shimmer in the air around the Moonchild and suddenly she could see the creature fully. It was a wisp of a thing and smaller than she'd originally thought, barely bigger than a toddler. The silver flashes she'd seen were from the Moonchild's faintly glittering skin and long tresses that looked as if they'd been spun from starlight.

Ros wasn't sure what to say, now that the creature had made itself visible to her. None of the tales had prepared her for this. She wiped her eyes, removing the traces of her breakdown, then bowed to the creature and said, "I am Rosalinde Adara Managold."

The Moonchild bowed in return. "Datura Whimsy, at your service. But please, just call me Whimsy."

"I'm pleased to make your acquaintance, Whimsy."

"I'm sure you are, when the other choice is the inside of a vuljasari. But not to worry—it can't harm you as long as you're in moonlight. A pact between the old gods and the new."

Rosalinde's brows raised. That was a bit of information she wished she'd known earlier. Such fae knowledge was scarce and viciously protected; in fact, she'd be surprised if there was anyone in Talabrih who knew that trick. Still, with a new moon above it wouldn't have helped her or the others.

"Do you have a way of knowing if my friends are okay?"

Whimsy nodded. "Is that your wish?"

Ros bit the inside of her cheek for a moment before answering, "No."

The Moonchild smiled. "Typical human. When you only get one wish, why waste it on something trivial, like the safety of others? So, what will you have, milady? Riches? Power? Or something sweeter, like, true love? Don't bother asking for a thousand wishes or someone to return from the dead—all magic has limits."

Ros shook her head. "I don't want any of those things."

"Well color me intrigued. Go on then, let's have it."

She could ask for her father to be returned. That made the most sense. But something about it didn't *feel* right. It was too easy.

Ros looked down at the drop of blood on her hand and thought back to what Cassian had said: *If the blood is active, he's alive.* As worried as she was about her father, there had been no change to the blood in her hand, so no change to his health.

Wishing him home wouldn't answer any of the questions about why he went missing in the first place, and it wouldn't stop whoever was out to get him from trying again.

"If I do not make a wish after you've agreed to grant one, what happens?"

Whimsy ran a pale blue tongue over sharp-looking teeth. After a moment, they said, "I told you before that I wouldn't harm you, and it remains true, for now. But do not test the patience of my folk. We do not grant boons often, but you've found me in a giving mood. I suggest you take your wish and question it no further."

Rosalinde said, "I mean no disrespect to your kindness or your gift, I simply hope to use it at a later time."

Whimsy paced back and forth by the edge of the stream for a moment, mumbling to themself. "...odd request...never before...will it hurt..."

"If it's too much trouble for you..." Ros began.

Whimsy flapped their hand in her direction and stopped pacing. "No, of course not. I'll give you the space of a moon. But if you have not used your wish by the next new moon, it is lost, and you will owe me something instead."

Ros knew better than to make a deal with a creature such as this, but she couldn't imagine any reason she wouldn't use her wish by then. She held out her empty hand and said, "Deal."

The Moonchild took her hand. Ros could feel heat in her palm where the creature touched her and when she let go, there was a sliver of white burned into her palm. She looked at it side by side with the blood droplet still clinging to her other hand.

Whimsy said, "Don't forget our deal, Rosalinde Adara Managold, because I will not. Tell no one of our encounter, dear girl, for I will know and be displeased if you do. If you choose to use your wish, touch the mark on your palm and I will come. But if you do not, I will come for something precious to you and claim it as my own."

And with that, they disappeared, leaving Ros in an empty, dark forest beside a dried-up creek bed where water clearly hadn't flowed for many, many moons.

THE SKY BEGAN to lighten a short while after Whimsy disappeared. Ros was certain a full night couldn't have passed, but perhaps time behaved differently inside the Moonchild's light. She walked Mercutio back through the trees the way she thought she'd come from. The forest was still dim, the trees blotting out the little bit of light above, but at least there was enough now to step with ease.

It took Ros the better part of the morning to find her way out of the forest. It hadn't seemed like she'd gone in very far last night, but this morning the woods stretched on before her endlessly.

But they did end, eventually. One moment she was in their shadows and the next she was stepping into the morning light. She had no way to know where the others were. Her best bet was to follow the blood in her palm until she found them or she found her father.

She mounted Mercutio and let the blood lead her.

SHE RAN into Florian around midday. He was atop his horse as it grazed, the reins tied around his body, fast asleep. Ros had never been more grateful to hear the snores of an egocentric man. She nudged Mercutio closer, letting him graze beside his companion.

"Florian," she whispered, trying not to alarm him.

He didn't budge.

She said his name again, more forcefully. Still he slumbered.

Finally, Ros yelled, "Wake up, you oaf!"

He jerked up, the reins catching him so he didn't fall off his horse. He blinked in the light, bleary eyes turning toward her. "Rosalinde? Thank the elements I've found you."

She laughed. "*You* found *me*?"

His cheeks reddened. "I've been searching for two days, my lady."

"Two days?" she asked. "But the attack was last night."

He shook his head. "Two nights ago."

Rosalinde shuddered, aghast that she'd lost so much time. How had her senses been so deceived within the forest? Was it Whimsy's work?

"Are you well, Princess? Did something happen to you?"

She nodded, though she was shaky at best. "Honestly, I don't know what happened." She considered telling him about Whimsy, but worried he would think her mad. And worse, she would earn Whimsy's displeasure, a fate she did not desire. Instead she asked, "How did you find me?"

"I followed your trail to that blasted forest, but lost you there. No matter where I steered myself inside it, I always ended up back at the same place. Romenia was here as well, circling these same woods, but when we couldn't find a way in, she left to report to the queen and seek reinforcements. You may think me silly for this, but I fear it is bewitched."

"I don't think you silly at all," she replied. Still, she didn't mention the Moonchild.

"When I felt myself growing weary, I strapped myself to Minola and hoped for the best."

"I didn't know you were a great tracker, my lord."

He nodded. "I've always loved the hunt. Never for the actual animals we track, but for the tracking itself. I'm quite good at it, but father says it's unbecoming of a nobleman."

"All due respect, but your father is wrong."

"Usually," Florian shrugged. "But I wouldn't suggest you tell him that."

Ros smiled. Seeing him without his normal boisterous countenance was refreshing. "Do you think you can find the others?"

Florian's red cheeks suddenly drained of color. "Yes, my lady. I'm certain I can find the survivors, if there are any."

Ros swallowed. "Tell me plainly what you mean by that."

"I reached my horse just as Zandor did, but I galloped away before I saw much more until I got far enough to turn and survey the scene. I know Zandor mounted his horse, but I didn't see him after that. Graeme was flying around the beast, avoiding the first attacks, but Will...well, he wasn't so lucky. He was trying to help Graeme, but ended up getting hit by the vuljasari."

She felt a lump rise into her throat. A member of her house, a young man there to help find her father...dead? No, she couldn't think that. She had to believe he was okay.

They rode in silence for a moment before she asked, "And the Night mage?"

Florian shook his head. "I don't know. I saw him disappearing and reappearing all over the place, in and out of existence in a flash."

"He's alive?"

"Yes. Or at least he was, before I left to come after you."

Ros let out the breath she was holding. She shouldn't care as much as she did. These men were equals, there to help find the king and win her heart. Ros needed to give them all the same chance to do so, and in her head, she knew that. But if she was being honest with herself, her heart already leaned toward the man she *couldn't* choose.

"Do you love him?"

The question caught her off guard and she jerked out of her thoughts. "What? Who?"

One side of Florian's mouth tilted up in a smile. "Cassian. That devil-tongued Night mage who can't seem to stay out of trouble. Do you love him?"

She stammered, "N-no, of course not."

"I'm no fool, Princess, even if I play one for the court. I've seen the way you are with him."

"Sir Florian, I treat all my suitors with the same courtesy—"

He waved away her words. "Of course you do, but that's not what I mean. It's more like, when he's around, you grow bolder, fiercer. Your very presence changes from an unsure future-ruler to the leader you were born to be. You seem like you're already the queen when he's by your side. Truthfully, that woman is the one we're all willing to follow, even if we've only seen glimpses so far."

Rosalinde didn't know how to respond. To know that such a thing was visible to the casual observer when she hadn't even considered it herself, well, it was disconcerting. After a moment, she managed, "I haven't given it much thought. He's the one I'm not supposed to choose."

"It would be a shock to the nobles," he chuckled.

Ros turned toward him, surprised at the genuine amusement on his face. This man was not the same as the one she knew. "You're different today."

He shrugged. "After that night, after we almost died, I figured there's no point pretending anymore. My parents have a facade they want from me, the way they think the heir to Fire house should behave. But I've seen the other men of Fire house, and I have no desire to be like them. I dislike the man they force me to be."

"I'm not fond of him either."

A deep, honest laugh boomed from Florian and Ros was surprised at the mirth in it. When it subsided, he said, "Glad that's out in the open. Now maybe we can get somewhere with this courtship. If you don't run away with the Night mage, anyway."

Ros smiled. "You know, my father wants me to choose Fire house."

"I know," he said. "He and my father have already spoken about it. I can't wait to see Father's expression when you don't choose me."

"You speak as if it's already decided."

He smirked at her. "It is, Rosalinde. Or at least it will be, when you admit it to yourself. But don't worry, I'll keep your secret and still help you find the king. I wasn't blustering when I said I was at your service, Highness. Nor when I told you of the changes I wish to make in my house. I don't have to be the king to make a difference."

"It would be easier."

"The easy road isn't always the right one. Your heart does not belong to me, and I doubt it ever could. Mine is not yours, either. A friendship, though, that is something we could grow, if Your Highness is willing."

"I am," she said, smiling. A moment of silence passed before she added, "Thank you," and meant it more than he could possibly know.

Sixteen

The camp was in chaos. Their packs and supplies were shredded, the food gone. While Florian searched for tracks or signs from the others, Ros rummaged through what was left of their belongings in the hopes of finding something worth salvaging.

"There are tracks leading east," he said when he rejoined her. "My guess is Zandor. He's the only one I know who made it to a horse."

Ros was only half listening. Instead, she stared at a dark stain in the grass. Blood. But whose?

"Hey," Florian said, putting his hand on her shoulder. He pulled her away from the spot and into his embrace. He held her for several minutes before saying, "It's not that much blood, okay? Just a little. It made a big mess for what was surely a small injury. Whoever it belonged to, it's not enough to kill them."

She pulled away from him and wiped her eyes. She swallowed back the tears threatening to overflow, taking on the practiced healer senses of her father. "I realize you're trying to soothe me, but my father is a Healer and I've been around this sort of thing before. A wound big enough to create a stain that large would cause someone to bleed out in a matter of minutes without proper help."

"Good thing I was here then, wasn't it? Someone had to save the day."

Ros turned at the sound of Cassian's voice. Unable to control her relief that he was okay, she threw herself against him, wrapping her arms around his waist and burying her face into his chest.

"I would've saved someone's life sooner if I'd known I'd get this sort of thanks."

Ros pulled back from him quickly, heat creeping up her neck as she realized what she'd done. She muttered, "Sorry."

"Don't be," he said.

"Is everyone okay then?" Florian asked, pretending he didn't just see the future queen throw herself at the Night Elementalist.

"William is," Cassian said. "The creature slashed him pretty badly, but was too distracted by Graeme to do much more. I took advantage of the distraction as well and grabbed Will, teleporting him back to the medical unit. Teague was able to patch him up and when I last saw him, he was resting comfortably, albeit disappointed to be out of competition for your hand, Princess. He's not coming back."

She nodded. "Understandably so. I'm just happy he's alright. What about the others?"

Cassian shook his head. "I didn't see what happened to Zandor. Graeme was gone when I came back from the medical wing."

"I found tracks over there," Florian said, pointing east. "If we head that way, I'm sure we'll find Zandor."

A look of surprise crossed Cassian's face, followed by a look of appreciation. "Good work. Anything left of the supplies?"

Ros held up the cup in her hands. "Not much else made it."

Cassian nodded, but it was clear he was distracted, like there was something else he wanted to ask but was afraid to.

"What is it?" Ros asked.

He glanced up at her and forced a smile. "Have you, um, seen any of my horses? I know it's unimportant in the grand scheme of things..." he trailed off.

"Oh, no," she said, her heart sinking. She hadn't considered that there were other lives out here aside from the people she was with, lives that Cassian cared about.

He rubbed a hand over his head. When he tried to smile, it was more like a wince. "They're not humans, but I love them all the same. They've always treated me well, even when people let me down.

"We know Mercutio and Minola are okay. We left

them grazing just beyond the trees," Florian said, forcing his voice to sound cheerful. "And Zandor jumped on one of them. I bet the other three ran."

"Did you see any tracks?"

Florian hesitated for a moment before whispering, "No. But that doesn't mean anything. The campsite was in shambles, so they would be easy to confuse for something else."

Cassian nodded. His voice was strained when he said, "It's getting late. Let's go find Zandor while we still can."

THE EVENING AMBLED on as they picked their way across the land. They'd moved quickly at first, the tracks wild but easy to follow. They found two of Cassian's horses as they traveled: Cicero, the one William had ridden, and Graeme's steed, Lady Macbeth. The beasts seemed as happy to see Cassian as he was relieved to see them. Ros had never had a strong bond with an animal, but she thought it seemed like a sign of good character to see how much they trusted him.

As they continued on and the ground changed from easy-to-read trampled grass to small rocks and stones, Zandor's trail fizzled to nothing. After a while, none of them could pick up even the faintest hint of where he might've gone.

Every step without success had Ros growing more agitated. She wanted to find Lyzandor—he'd been a friend of hers for years—but she also wanted to find her father. With Zandor's trail going cold and her father's blood still on her hand, her mind went back and forth over which one they should pursue.

Still, they kept going in their pursuit of the missing young man and Ros kept her mouth shut about the futility of it versus chasing a sure lead. Their pace was slow as they were careful not to endanger the horses twisting a leg amongst the rocks. Despite the dangers, no one wanted to be the one to suggest stopping.

Finally, Ros gave in and said, "It's no use. We've lost his trail, and we're not going to find it again stumbling around in the near-darkness. Let's make camp."

Cassian pointed up the rocky incline. "Looks like there's a cave up there. Probably a safer bet than out in the open again."

They made their way up the side of the mountain and stopped at the mouth of the cave. While Cassian secured the horses and Ros watered them, Florian checked inside the cave for dangers.

"Nothing here," he said when he returned. "It doesn't go back very far."

"That's the first bit of good luck we've had today," Cassian said.

Rosalinde's stomach grumbled and she placed her hand over her empty belly. "I don't suppose either of you was able to find some food?"

In the blink of an eye, Cassian disappeared.

"What the—" Florian started.

Cassian reappeared before he could finish his sentence. His arms were laden with food. Ros removed her cloak and spread it on the ground so he could lay out their feast of fruits, cheese, and bread. He'd even managed to fill his pockets with a handful of nuts and a couple carrots.

"Can't you flit around in the dark and find Zandor?" Florian asked as he bit into a pear. "I'm ready to be done with this so we can return to the bigger mission."

Cassian smirked. "That's not how my gift works."

"How would I know?" Florian shrugged. "You're pretty secretive about it."

"After what happened last time a Night Elementalist tried to be part of the kingdom, can you blame me?"

Rosalinde's brows furrowed. The last time a Night mage came out of hiding, it was Cassian's mother, but nothing happened to her. She didn't win the Great Match of her year and she left, but that was it. She disappeared into legend, and no one had seen another Night mage until Cassian showed up.

Florian looked as confused as Ros felt as he said, "I don't know what you're talking about."

Cassian squinted at Florian in disbelief, but his expression changed when he caught Ros wearing the same look. "You really don't know?"

Ros shook her head. "I've heard about your mother's time in the Great Match, but—"

"My mother? No," he said, shaking his head. "I'm talking about my brother."

"I didn't know you had a brother. You said you were Ombretta's only heir."

"I am, now," Cassian said.

"I'm sorry for your loss," Florian said, "Forgive me if it's calloused to ask, but since you brought it up, are you able to tell us what happened to him?"

"He was murdered after his time in the Great Match four years ago," Cassian said.

Ros slowly shook her head. "I don't want to diminish his memory, but there was no competitor from the Night house four years ago. You're the first Dark mage the kingdom has seen since your mother."

Cassian pressed his lips into a tight line. After a moment, he said, "I'm sure it's difficult to remember every contestant. His name was Gaius."

"I definitely don't remember each one, but I guarantee if there had been someone from the Night house, I wouldn't have forgotten them," she said.

Florian said, "You may not have realized it, dear friend, but your presence sent every house into chaos. Every nobleman in the kingdom has been panicking since your arrival. If there had been another Night mage, especially in the Great Match, we would remember."

"I don't understand," Cassian said. "My mother told me about his death. I mean, she didn't give me all the details, but I saw how much she hurt when we said goodbye to him."

Ros knew there hadn't been a Night mage anywhere near the castle in twenty-five years, but instead of saying so, she said, "Maybe something happened before the Match. We can ask around when we get back. Maybe someone will have heard."

Cassian nodded, but his eyes were clouded with confusion. He muttered, "I'm going to turn in. Wake me when it's my turn to keep watch."

When his eyes closed, the night seemed to grow darker around them, putting an end to all conversation about the mysterious missing Night mage.

THE MORNING WAS cool as they set off, trying to catch a hint of Zandor's whereabouts. By mid-afternoon, the weather had grown as warm as their tempers while they snapped at one another in frustrated tones.

But when Florian spotted a break in the rocks that looked like a horse may have slipped, everything changed. They were back on track and eager to find their missing companion, hopefully unharmed.

When they stopped for a water break and to give the horses a rest, they were still in surprisingly high spirits. Florian was telling a bawdy story about the first set of breasts he ever saw, sending water spewing from Rosalinde's mouth at a particularly colorful bit. As he reached the climax of his story, his words were cut off as a scream sliced through the seemingly empty land around them. They turned, looking for the source of the sound.

"There," Florian said, pointing to a boulder fifty yards ahead.

Cassian disappeared, reappearing an instant later beside the massive stone. Ros watched him put his hands above his head before stepping around the boulder out of sight.

She couldn't see what was happening, but she knew she needed to get to him right then. She slid off Mercutio and threw his reins to Florian. "Don't endanger the horses. Follow when you can."

Ros called upon her gift. She felt the water surging to her, begging to rise up and overwhelm her and the land around her. That was the problem with having a gift like Tsunami: it was wild and uncontrollable, always seeking to consume and destroy.

But Ros was focused, her mind and heart on Cassian. Her gift could not overwhelm her when she was already consumed by the way she felt about him. The water rose under her feet, rushing her toward the boulder. It moved with her, leaving the ground behind her wet, but not flooded.

When she reached the place where Cassian had disappeared, less than a minute had passed. He was standing there with his hands still raised. Zandor was on the ground ahead of him, but Ros couldn't see what was wrong with him. She peered around the boulder until her eyes landed on the source of the trouble: Graeme.

He floated a foot off the ground and seemed to crackle with energy. It wasn't like the elemental power he possessed. No, this was dark magic—but nothing like the darkness that Cassian controlled. She could *feel* malice sparking in the air around him. Shadows seemed to creep from tiny fissures in his skin and she knew immediately what was wrong. Whatever was happening with the darkness, whatever had taken her in the great hall, that evil that Cassian had pulled out of Elaina in the medical unit...it was here. It had been festering in Graeme since the vuljasari attack, maybe longer, and it wasn't giving up as easily as it had before.

She slipped back behind the rock, hoping he hadn't noticed her, but she'd barely moved when she heard, "And where do you think you're going, Princess?"

With a curse, Ros stepped back into their view. She said, "Graeme, this isn't you."

The thing inside Graeme barked out a laugh. "Oh, how perceptive. Or at least that's what you're hoping, right? Because what would it mean if this *was* Graeme? That would make you a fool, aye."

"Leave her out of this," Cassian said, trying to step between her and Graeme. "We can work something out."

"That is truly precious. A Night mage with a noble heart. But alas, I've seen what you can do and I have no use for it. Be gone."

Graeme flicked his hand and threw Cassian against the rocks near Zandor. Ros let out a yelp, her hand flying to her mouth, when she saw the way Cassian landed. There was no way he wasn't injured; she wasn't positive, but Ros thought she could see the bone jutting out of his twisted ankle.

She turned back to Graeme, eyes narrowed. Her powers surged through her, electrifying every cell of her body with the need to be used against this foe. She felt it building in her fingertips, aching to escape and wreak havoc on the evil around her.

But she held it back. Barely, but that was enough for now.

"What are you?" she asked.

Graeme shrugged. "Just a passenger, darling, looking for the right host. And if I'm being honest, I'm not wild about this one. It seemed fine until I tried it out two nights ago against that vuljasari. Turns out all he can do is fly around. It looks far better than it really is. I'm looking for something a little more intense. Like, I don't know, Tsunami-strength power."

"Forget it," she spat. "I'll never let you take control of me."

"Pretty sure you will, actually. If not, I'm going to kill your lover-boy."

Ros told herself not to look at him, willing her eyes to stay focused on Graeme, but felt them slip to Cassian anyway. She only glanced at him for a second, but it was enough to confirm Graeme's words.

She took a deep breath, willing herself to stay calm. "If you took me, would you give your word to let the others go?"

He shrugged. "As long as you gave yourself fully, they'd be of no further use to me."

A flicker of movement behind Graeme caught Rosalinde's eyes, but this time she refused to look. She knew it was Florian, it had to be, and she needed to give him as much of a distraction as she could for whatever he was doing.

"Why do you need me?"

Graeme sighed. "That's really none of your business."

"It's my body."

"I don't care about your *body*. I want your power. It's sitting there, untapped, wasted on the likes of you. But in my hands, we could be the strongest mage in Talabrih."

"Maybe I'm already the strongest."

Graeme laughed, a vicious crackle of sound accompanied by a wisp of shadow floating from his mouth. "I have no doubt you could be, if you weren't so afraid to release the waters churning within you. You'll never be anything until you do."

She bit the inside of her cheek, as if considering his words. "But you can make me great."

"No, Rosalinde," Cassian said. "You can't."

"He's right though, isn't he? I'll never really be able to use or control these powers until I learn what they can do when they're fully unleashed."

"You know I'm right. Come here and let's end this, together."

She took a step toward Graeme, ignoring the pained

yells from Cassian as she did. Another step and she reached out her hands. "Ready?"

Graeme reached for her just as Florian sprang up behind him. He zapped Graeme with a bolt of lightning so strong Ros could hear his teeth rattling together. Somehow, Graeme managed to move his hand, to call on his Air power, and send Florian flying to the ground like the others.

He turned his twitching head back toward Rosalinde and said, "You should be ashamed, Princess. I thought we'd reached an understanding."

"We have," she breathed. "It was a misunderstanding, a poor attempt by the Fire mage. Please, let them live."

"How ever can I trust you now?" he asked.

"They're all defeated. What else is there for me to do?"

Graeme shrugged. "With those pesky children out of the way, I suppose we can still finish our bargain."

He grabbed her wrists as dark wisps poured from Graeme's mouth, nose, ears, and even his eyes. She felt his grip weaken as the darkness left him. Graeme's body fell to the ground, the stench of burnt flesh clinging to him. The smell stuck to the back of Rosalinde's throat—sour and cloying, a smell she would never get out of her mouth again—but there was nothing she could do. The darkness was already pooling inside her. It had claimed her for its own.

She took one final breath as herself before she felt the darkness take control.

Seventeen

Rosalinde looked down at the two men on the ground to her right. She could see Cassian and Zandor, knew it was them, but this new, dark part of her only saw them as the enemy. She could feel the darkness twisting her powers toward them.

"You said you'd let them go," she said, through a voice that wasn't entirely hers anymore.

"I said they would be of no use to me," the darkness replied.

"You can't hurt them."

"I can and I will. Besides, you'll feel better once they're gone. No one to know what happened to you, how easily you gave in."

But it didn't matter. Cassian took away the reason for their argument when he grabbed Zandor's wrist and disappeared.

"A pity," the darkness said. "I was really looking forward to killing that little darkling. He had pizazz."

Ros pushed against the darkness riding in her body, trying to take control. She could feel it spreading out, reaching tendrils of darkness into the deepest part of her. She cleared her mind, trying to put up blockades to keep it from worming into her thoughts.

"You're just upset about not killing him because you know he'll be your downfall."

"You give the boy more credit than he's due. He's weak."

When the darkness laughed, it came out of her mouth. It was *her* chest that shook with the foul thing's delight, *her* body beginning to respond to its commands. But by all the elements, she wasn't giving in without a fight.

"He's stronger than you'll ever be."

"You don't know him like I do, no matter how much you might think you love him. He's always been soft, easy to control, too afraid to do what's necessary."

"Don't pretend you know anything about him," she said.

She saw a flicker at the corner of her eye and turned just in time to see Cassian flash out of existence, Graeme's body in tow. She looked to Florian's body—or where it had been. While she was arguing with the darkness, Cassian must've come back for him. In her heart, she was certain he would return for her as well. She needed to give him more time.

"He can have their bodies. I only need this one."

The darkness surged within her, pressing against the frail boundaries she'd put in place.

Pathetic, it thought, taking over her mind. *You're as weak-willed as he is.*

Rosalinde held tightly to the sliver of herself still there, the part he hadn't yet been able to take. Without reasoning, without thought, she knew what that piece was and why he hadn't been able to control it like the rest of her: it was built of tiny moments from everyone she knew, everyone who had made her who she was. It was made of love and light, things this villain didn't know how to use.

She clung to her mother's bedside whispers when she was a child, playing dolls with Elsabet, visiting the sick with her father. She dug her nails into memories of sneaking out with Larkin, kissing boys behind the stables, getting sick from too much bad ale with the twins a couple years older than her, Sascha and Sebastian. She thought of nights with Alaric and knowing she was falling in love with him, but being unable to do anything about it.

Then, to her surprise, she found a bit of Cassian in there. She remembered the way he caught her when she tripped on the stairs and realized that she had started falling for him even then. She remembered the way he frightened her simply by saying who he was, the way danger seemed to surround him like a cloak—but that was all it was, something he could take on and off when needed. Underneath, he was kind. He cared about others, like her father. He built her up, like her mother. Like Elsabet, he challenged her, made her better. He was as much a part of her now as any of the others.

Stop that, the darkness thought.

Ros didn't know what she'd done, only that she'd been thinking about Cassian. She focused on him, remembering the way it felt the first time he'd teleported her through the darkness. He'd put his hand on her waist and moved her into his world, giving her a glimpse no outsider had seen before. There were so many colors, so much more than she expected.

"I said to stop," the darkness said.

It pulled at her thoughts, trying to dismantle them from the edges. She felt it scratching at them, but no matter what it did, she held firm. She would hold onto this last bit of herself until the breath left her lungs for the final time.

She felt a hand clamp around her wrists and looked up to see Cassian's dark eyes staring down at her. He whispered her name, shaking her as he did, but she couldn't seem to form words anymore. She couldn't make her mouth move, couldn't do anything but hold onto that tiny core that was the last part of her that hadn't been consumed.

"You can't have her," he growled.

She felt the darkness recoil at his words. Somehow, she knew it wasn't from fear, simply surprise. Though she couldn't make words on her own, she could hear the darkness say, "You're too late, Cassian. This one is mine."

"I will not lose her to you or anyone else."

The force in Cassian's voice would've taken her breath away, if the darkness wasn't controlling that, too. She felt him pulling at the darkness inside her, winding his elemental magic into her to rip at the power that was holding her hostage, just as he had taken it out of her in the castle when it tried to control her the first time.

But this was too much, even for him. This wasn't the tiny part of every person that leaned toward evil, this was a being made of malevolence that now lived inside her body. He might be able to get it out of her, he might even be able to consume it, like he had the smaller pieces, but even without fully understanding his powers she knew he wouldn't be able to control it for long. In the end, it would swallow him up and leave nothing but a husk.

She had to warn him, had to stop him. Maybe while the darkness was distracted with Cassian, she had a chance. From the tiny part of her mind that still belonged to her, Rosalinde held tight to her love that was blooming for Cassian. She fed it with her thoughts, built it up, and pushed it out from herself. She watched that love spread through her mind, *felt* it moving through her body just as she'd felt the darkness when it had taken control.

"What are you doing?" the darkness thought.

She wasn't sure, but it almost sounded nervous. Ros didn't answer, just pushed more love out into herself, letting it flood through her until she felt her stomach doing somersaults at the mere thought of Cassian's strange, dark eyes.

The darkness slithered out of her as quickly as it had entered. Cassian reached for it, but it slipped between his fingers, a black smoke that smelled of decay.

"You haven't seen the last of me, Princess," it said. "I *will* have your power."

"You'll never have her," Cassian said.

As it faded on the breeze, Ros heard a faint laugh as it said, "We'll see about that, little hollow boy. We'll see."

"Hollow boy?" she asked.

Cassian's face had gone pale. He dropped to his knees. His eyebrows were raised, his mouth ajar, but it was the sadness in his eyes that caught Rosalinde off guard. There was more pain in those eyes than Ros had ever seen.

She knelt in front of him and put her hands on each side of his face, drawing his gaze to her. "I'm here. How can I help?"

"Gaius," he whispered, tears beginning to trickle at the corners of his eyes. "It-it can't be. He died. Mother told me..."

"Gaius?" she repeated. "Your brother?"

Cassian nodded. "He always called me that—*hollow boy*. That's what my name means. He always said Mother named me that because that's how she felt when I was born. That I wasn't wanted."

His words were a punch in the gut. As much as she

and her sister fought, Ros couldn't imagine saying something like that to Elsabet. It was hurtful and cruel, the
kind of thing your family was supposed to *protect* you
from.

Ros stroked his face with her thumb from cheekbone
to jaw. She wanted to comfort him, but couldn't imagine
what he was feeling right now. "It was probably just a
trick. The darkness is trying to weaken you."

Cassian's eyes were on her, but when he spoke it was
as if he was looking straight through. "I wasn't sorry that
he died. He was a terrible brother, a terrible person. I
swore to myself I would never be like him."

"You're not," she said. "You're nothing like him."

"How do you know?" he asked, his eyes meeting hers
in a way that seemed to plead for her to give him proof
that he wasn't the same as Gaius.

"Look at what you did today," she said. "You have the
ability to teleport. You could've escaped all of this. But
you didn't. You saved the others, risking yourself every
time you returned. And you came back for me."

"Anyone would've—"

"No, not anyone," she said, cutting him off. Ros
pressed her moon-scarred palm against his chest. "Your
brother wouldn't have. You don't have to tell me
anything else about him for me to know that. If that
thing really is Gaius, I felt him in me. I know who he is,
and you are nothing like him."

Cassian put his hands over hers where they rested
against his face. "Thank you."

Ros felt heat rise into her cheeks as he looked at her. The gap between them seemed to shrink, though neither of them moved. Cassian's lips curled at the edges in a tentative smile that seemed shy and knowing at the same time.

Her stomach flipped again as her feelings flooded back to the front of her mind. The affection for this man, the love she'd been afraid to admit, was the very thing that had protected her from Gaius.

She stared at his cheekbones, at the slope of his nose, the silhouette of a beard on his jaws. Ros tried to look anywhere but his lips, but of course that's where her eyes inevitably went. There was something mesmerizing about them and once her eyes landed there, she couldn't look away. As she watched, begging them to draw nearer, she saw them start moving instead.

"I want to kiss you," Cassian breathed.

"Okay," she said, still staring at his perfect mouth.

His smile grew ever so slightly, but he said, "I can't though, no matter how much I want to. Not until this is over and you choose me."

"What? Why?" she asked, finally meeting his eyes.

"I can't let this get out of hand. I know how I feel about you, but you've got a big decision to make and you need to be thinking clearly. I want you to pick me, Ros, but I need to know you're doing it for the right reasons and not just because we went through something traumatic together."

"It isn't because of that," she protested. "I mean, yes,

that definitely made me realize how I'm feeling, but—"

He shook his head. "I want our first kiss to be the day I know you're never going to kiss anyone but me, forever."

The words gave her pause. Even her parents kissed other people. It was accepted, expected even, for them to take lovers. If he was saying he didn't want that, wanted to only be with her...did that mean he loved her? That he wanted to love *only* her, forever? She'd always assumed she would have an open relationship like those before and hadn't given any consideration to what monogamy would be like. She wasn't opposed to either way of life— she'd just never imagined she would have the chance for a love match, and the best she could hope for was comfort in the arms of those willing to warm her bed without having her heart. Was she ready to be with Cassian, and only him, for the rest of her life? And if love was truly possible for her, was Cassian the one?

He stood up, not giving her the chance to dwell on the question further. Reaching down a hand, he helped her to her feet. "Come on, we need to go."

"Where are we going?"

"To finish our quest, Princess. We still need to find the king."

She nodded. "We'll need supplies and a place to rest. We might also need more help than we thought."

"I have someone in mind."

"Who?"

"My mother."

Eighteen

Rosalinde wasn't sure what she was expecting from the Night house, but this wasn't it. She'd imagined massive black spires and a draw-bridge over a moat filled with spider-fish, maybe the occasional head on a spike. She should have known better after getting to know Cassian, but years of tall tales about a mysterious house that had all but disappeared from history had built a villain's fairytale castle in her head and it wasn't until they were standing at the fence that she realized how wrong those stories had been.

It was more a cottage than a manor, and certainly not a castle, covered in flowering vines. There was a wisp of smoke coming from the chimney, curling lazily into the sky. They passed through the small wooden gate that squeaked as Cassian opened it and walked up the stone flagstones to the rounded door.

Cassian didn't bother knocking. He pushed through the door and called, "Mother, I'm home."

Ros smiled, unable to hold back. There was such joy in his tone, such honest delight in being back at his familial house, that she felt it pulsing from him in waves.

She heard a woman calling his name from somewhere farther in the house and a moment later, a tall woman with thick black curls came bolting into the room. She threw her arms around his neck and hugged him fiercely, saying, "I'm so happy you're home. Tell me everything that happened."

It wasn't until she released him that she seemed to notice Rosalinde. Like her son, she was tall, with black hair and dark eyes, high cheekbones, and startling good looks. Also like her son, she wore her emotions on her face, and right now she was wearing a look of surprise.

"Good day," Ros said, dipping into a curtsy.

"Forgive me," she breathed, bowing low just as Cassian always did. "You took me by surprise. I didn't expect the future queen in my home today."

"I apologize for any inconvenience it causes," Ros said.

"Inconvenience? Of course not, Your Highness. It is my honor."

Cassian rolled his eyes. "Can we please stop with the formalities? There's a lot we need to talk about and we don't really have the time for you two to feel each other out."

His mother smirked. "Bold of you to speak that way."

"She's not stuffy like the other nobles, Mother. She can handle it."

"I wasn't talking about her," Ombretta said. "That's no way to speak to your mother."

Cassian broke into a wide grin that his mother quickly mirrored. "You're right and I'm terribly sorry. Dearest Mother, high ruler of Night house, Lady of Darkness, I'd like you to meet Ros."

Ombretta flipped her hair over her shoulder and said, "That's so much better, darling."

When they laughed together, Ros felt like she was missing out on the joke. Still, she was glad to see that after all that had happened only minutes ago, Cassian was still able to feel something other than heartache.

"Lady of Darkness," Ros repeated. "Very intimidating."

"Thank you," Ombretta said.

"It would probably be more effective if you didn't smile so much," Cassian said.

"What fun would that be?" she asked.

Ombretta turned and walked through the open doorway behind her. Cassian grabbed Rosalinde's hand and pulled her into the next room and out a side door that led into a walled garden. There were vines growing above and all around them, flowers and bushes, and beautiful blossoming trees at the corners of the grounds.

Ros was entranced by the place, knowing the amount of work that must've gone into it.

"Your garden is lovely," Ros said.

Ombretta waved a hand toward some seats. As they sat, she said, "Oh, it's nothing. Certainly not when compared with a Botanical mage like yourself."

"Oh, no," Ros said, shaking her head, "I don't have my mother's gift. My sister does, but I ended up between houses with Tsunami power."

"Right, that's your primary. But you must have an ability with plants, don't you? I would imagine it would be easy for you, with your mother's substantial powers."

Ros furrowed her brows. "I'm sorry, I'm not sure what you're talking about."

Ombretta turned to Cassian and clucked her tongue. "I thought you were going to show her how to access her full range. How do you expect to woo her without..."

She trailed off when she looked down and saw their joined hands. Cassian said, "I planned to teach her, yes, but things haven't gone how I expected. That's why we're here."

Ombretta nodded. "Spill it."

Cassian squeezed Rosalinde's hand and said, "First, Ros, I want you to understand what we're talking about. I'll explain everything in more detail when I can, but the basics are this: as an Elementalist, you can access more than one gift. I know it isn't taught that way and everyone focuses on their one big thing, but that's just a failure in our system. You have Tsunami, as you know, but there's more that you haven't tapped into yet."

His words clicked into place in her mind, filling in the blanks about him. "I thought it was strange, the way you use more than one gift. But with everything else happening, it never occurred to me to ask. At the opening ceremonies when I made you mad, you said you could teach me true power. You teleport, but you also covered the stadium in darkness, and you absorbed the darkness in the hall. Then you awakened the blood—and I *know* it was you, not me—but you didn't want anyone to realize you were doing it because of the mistrust already there. You were using multiple gifts this whole time."

Cassian nodded. "No one realizes it because no one understands what a Night mage can do."

"Even us, at times," Ombretta said. "We have no one to guide us, so we work to figure out our powers as best we can. We try to share our knowledge with the others of Night house—"

"There has been no record of any living mage from Night house in our current age until you arrived at the castle twenty-five years ago, yet here you both sit," Ros interrupted. "Though it has been hundreds of years since anyone has seen your people, I get the impression those numbers are inaccurate. How many of you are there?" Ros asked.

"We are few and far between," Ombretta said.

Ros noted the careful way Ombretta gave a non-answer. "But not as rare as you'd have the rest of Talabrih believe. Why is that?"

"I'm not sure what you mean," the Lady of Darkness said.

"Why do you hide away from the other houses, guarding your gifts so secretively?"

Ombretta's dark eyes glinted, revealing a little more of the shadow under her smile. Perhaps she was not as friendly as she wanted Ros to believe.

"It's the only way to keep safe. But that's not something a royal of Water house could ever understand."

"You haven't given me a chance to."

"Believe me, you're not the first I've tried to tell."

My father, Ros thought. His Great Match had come down to Ombretta and her mother. What secrets had she revealed to him, and how many of those did he still carry?

"I can't begin to know what happened between you and my father—"

"Don't, please," Ombretta said. "That was a lifetime ago."

"Things could still be repaired between our houses," Ros said.

"Too much has happened; the blood of our past cannot be unspilled."

"We can try," Ros said. "Here, now, we could forge beyond history and search for a way forward, together."

"Our house has tried and tried again, until there weren't enough of us left to keep sacrificing to a lost cause. I will not lose a son to such foolishness."

Ros asked, "Is that what happened to Gaius? Or did he do it to himself by pushing his gift too far?"

Ombretta's expression was enough to tell Ros what she needed to know. The woman recovered quickly, but her face had already given her away. She *knew.*

"Ros, please," Cassian said, shocked at her indiscretion. "I know we're in a hurry, but have some tact. He was her *son.*"

"She already knows," Ros said, nodding toward Ombretta.

Cassian looked between the two women, his brows furrowed. After a few seconds, he stopped looking at Ros and focused on his mother. He shook his head in denial, his heart breaking for the second time that day.

"Let me explain," Ombretta said.

Cassian jumped up. "Explain? You told me he was dead!"

"He was, in every way that mattered."

"But I talked to him. I *felt* him."

"That thing is not your brother," Ombretta said. "It's all that's left of him. Anger, bitterness, a desire for vengeance."

"Maybe you didn't know Gaius as well as you think, because that sounds like him even before this happened."

"I have no delusions about your brother. He was born with a darkness in him that has nothing to do with the elements. That's why I worked with him so often and gave him so much of my time—I wanted to spare him from the misery he was building for himself."

"Tell me what happened," Cassian said.

Ombretta shook her head. "I don't want you to know this pain."

"I'm not a child anymore. You can't protect me now, just like you couldn't protect Gaius."

"I wasn't trying to protect Gaius," she whispered. "I was trying to protect everyone else...from him."

There was a long moment of silence while her words hung in the air between them before Cassian finally sat down at her feet and took her hand. It was such an intimate gesture that Ros wasn't sure she should still be there. But she had to stay. She needed to know everything she could about Gaius if they were going to defeat him. Whatever he was, whatever his motive, he had something to do with her missing father. Maybe Gaius was too far gone, but Ros could still save the king.

"You know how he was," Ombretta said, swallowing hard. "Callous. Easy to anger. But he was clever and cunning, too. He was driven. Gaius was so desperate to bring prominence to Night house that he was unhinged by that ambition."

"Which is why he was entering the Great Match. To make alliances with the other houses."

Ros pressed her lips together. She already knew that Gaius hadn't participated in the Great Match four years ago, but Cassian had been fed the story by his mother, and she had to be the one to take it away.

Ombretta shook her head. "I told you that because I thought it would keep you safe. If you thought the other houses were against us, you wouldn't want anything to do with them."

"He never went to the castle," Cassian breathed.

He glanced at Ros. She tried to give him a meaningful look, but there was so much hurt on his face. Finding out that his brother was still alive—at least somewhat—and now learning that his mother had lied to him? Ros couldn't imagine how broken he must feel right now.

"No. And I was glad he didn't. Revealing ourselves to the other houses has always been a mistake. That's why I didn't want you to go either, despite your insistence. I thought you'd come back alone, ready to let go of the other houses once and for all."

"I was so angry," Cassian said. "The fact that Ros is by my side is a miracle after the way I've behaved. I've carried rage over Gaius' death with me these last four years. I went to the Great Match to prove to everyone that we aren't afraid of them, that we could be so much more than they think of us. But it was all based on lies."

"You are more," Ros said, grasping his hand.

"You must think me a fool," he said, his eyes searching hers.

Ros shook her head, trying to chase away those dark thoughts from him. She thought him many things, but not that. Hearing all that had happened, she now understood where his anger came from and why it was so hard to get him to open up. If anything, this just proved how wonderful he was, that he was able to overcome the lies he'd believed for so long.

Cassian took a deep breath and let it out slowly. "If Gaius didn't go to the Great Match, where was he?"

"He went on a quest, trying to find the place where our power is strongest."

"That's absurd," Cassian said.

"Not really," Ros said, wincing at the way her voice cut into this moment. But she needed to share the things she knew, if they were all going to be on the same page. "The old scrolls at the palace library mention places in this world, Cradles, they call them, where our powers are born. They say an Elementalist's powers will grow stronger there, but that's about all they say. The scrolls aren't specific, at least not in a way today's scholars can understand. But the Cradles are definitely out there."

"I've found two of them," Ombretta said.

"Two of them?" Ros asked, brows rising.

She nodded. "One for Fire, one for Night."

"How did you find Fire?" Ros asked.

Ombretta said, "With help from a Fire mage."

Cassian shot his mother a look that Ros couldn't read. He took a deep breath and let it out slowly. When he spoke, his tone was one of defeat. "When I tell you this, you become one of three people in this world who know the truth. The other two are sitting in this garden with you. Can I trust you with this secret?"

"Yes," Ros breathed.

Ombretta said, "Cassian, please don't—"

"We've kept enough secrets, Mother. It's time to let someone in."

"I tried," Ombretta said, her voice cracking. "I told her father and he betrayed me."

Both Ros and Cassian's gazes darted to Ombretta. She looked back at Ros, defiant. But it was Cassian who said, "She's not her father. She has his blood, but she is her own person and I trust her. If you can't, at least trust me."

Ombretta nodded. "Always."

Cassian turned to Ros and said, "Night mages are made from two opposing gifts: a Fire house Light mage and a Water house Blood Healer. And either of those two magics mixed with an existing Night mage will always produce Night magic."

"But that doesn't make sense," Ros said.

"It does, if you understand the combinations," Ombretta said.

"I was obsessed with them growing up," Cassian said. "I spent hours figuring up different combinations. There are so many things we leave untapped with our magic, Ros. We could do so much more if people would be open to exploring more than the basic constructs."

Ombretta shook her head. "You were both so interested in what *could* be. Neither of you were willing to consider that it had already been done, that things are this way now because it's the only way magic survives."

"Maybe it shouldn't survive," Cassian said.

Part of Ros thought he was right. Magic caused trouble. It was dangerous, separated the classes, and turned people into power-hungry monsters like Gaius. But then she thought of how Teague had healed those people in the arena, the way her mother's flowers bloomed in the royal garden, how she was able to call forth water for the thirsty.

"Magic can be helpful and beautiful, if it's used the right way. We just need to figure out how to keep it from misuse."

"Starting with Gaius," Cassian growled.

Ros looked down at the drop of blood on her palm. Defeating Gaius was important to Cassian, but she still needed to find her father. As if reading her thoughts, Cassian said, "It's all connected. Your father's disappearance and my brother's return from the dead."

"Your father is missing?" Ombretta asked.

Ros wasn't positive, but it sounded like true concern in her voice. "Since the opening ceremony. We think someone is making a play for the throne."

Ombretta ran a hand over her eyes. With a sigh, she said, "I have no love for your father after all that happened between us, but he is a good king and I swore an oath to him a long, long time ago. So, tell me how I can help."

Nineteen

The whinny of a horse woke Rosalinde the next morning. She looked out the window to see Cassian standing in the yard with six horses around him. There was a broad smile across his face, and his relief was clear in the set of his shoulders and the relaxed way he stood.

"He taught them the way home," Ombretta said as she came up behind Ros. "No matter where they are, how lost they may get, they always find their way back to him."

"That's a beautiful bond," Ros said.

Ombretta nodded. "I don't know if a bond like that can extend to people, but if it could, Cassian would be the one to find out. When you know him, when you *really* know him, it's impossible not to be drawn back to him."

The words struck Ros, sending a pang through her

chest. She knew there was so much about the Night mage that she didn't know yet, but she felt a bond with him, as if their hearts knew each other even while they themselves did not. She desperately hoped that no matter what happened, they would continue to be drawn back together.

AFTER CASSIAN TOOK care of his horses and the three had something to eat, they filed out of Ombretta's cottage with a tentative plan in mind. They'd spent the evening before getting their bearings, working through what they knew about the abduction, the darkness, and conspiracies about who could be after the throne. To save the king, they'd need to trust each other and work together—something Ombretta seemed reluctant to do despite offering her help. The one thing they knew for sure was if they were going to rescue King Tancred, they would need to stop the darkness, or whoever was controlling it.

Ros wasn't convinced anyone was controlling Gaius. From what she'd felt of him, he was hungry for power and control. King-napping seemed like an easy way to get the things he desired. Then again, she couldn't figure out why he would wait until now to do it. If he'd been gone four years, what had kept him from seeking out the king before now?

She didn't bother asking Cassian or Ombretta their

opinion about it. They'd made it clear they thought Gaius was being controlled, manipulated from outside sources, and despite the dark desires they'd seen in him in the years at his side, they thought he could be rescued and rehabilitated. Though she disagreed, she refused to be the one to take that hope from Cassian. If that was what he needed to believe, she'd let him hold onto it as long as possible and do her best to keep her thoughts from showing.

Ombretta wanted to go to the Night Cradle, where she thought Gaius would have found his new powers, and where he might return if he needed to recharge his strength. Though she refused to say why, Ombretta believed Gaius would need to seek the Cradle regularly while he was incorporeal.

She instructed Cassian where she wanted him to teleport them, giving him a location he remembered that was near the Cradle. Ros wondered why she didn't transfer them to the site herself, until Cassian explained that his mother had never quite mastered the ability. She could move about in smoke form, as they'd seen Gaius do and as the old stories claimed she did the night her Great Match ended, but she couldn't move from place to place like her youngest son. Even with those who mastered more than a primary gift, some things were still easier to do if you were predisposed, it seemed.

Cassian teleported them to the top of a hill where stone ruins lay around them. There an archway above them—the only thing still standing—and everything was covered in purple moss and dark mushrooms speckled with silver.

"What is this place?" Ros asked, her breath catching in her throat as she stared out at the abandoned beauty around her.

"It's the Night castle," Ombretta said.

Ombretta walked through the broken stones as if it were an elaborately decorated hallway. Ros could easily imagine her gliding through elegant hallways, dressed in rich clothing and drenched in jewels, ruling the Night house. Everything about her said she was noble, even if her blood did not.

Ombretta continued, "This place housed the original Night Elementalists, before they were eradicated."

"What are you talking about? Prior to your family, there was only one other known Night Elementalist in the last few hundred years. Those who came before vanished."

Ombretta shook her head. "In the history you're taught, maybe. We're rare, certainly, but that's only because most prefer to hide out as non-magicals to avoid being hunted by the other houses."

"This doesn't make sense," Ros whispered.

"The truth isn't always pleasant, Princess," Cassian said.

Ombretta led them out of the ruins and down the hill toward the woods. "I thought I could change things if I were queen. That's why I went, you know. It was a longshot, but when I met your father...I had hope. As a

Blood healer, I thought he might relate more to the Night house than anyone else could. I thought he might understand me."

Ros opened her mouth to ask a question, but something entirely different came out before she could stop herself: "Did you love him?"

In the following silence, Ros was glad she was behind Ombretta and couldn't see her face. The quiet stretched on for several minutes before Ombretta said, "I don't know. You could've asked me the same question a hundred times over the last twenty-five years and received a different answer each time. Sometimes I thought I did, but sometimes I hated him. Mostly, I don't think I knew him well enough to feel either of those things."

Ros felt her words digging their way into her bones. It hadn't been a week yet, but she'd already felt the same things toward Cassian. Just days ago, she was promising herself she would get rid of him as soon as possible, but now she didn't want to consider what her life would be like without him. Maybe it was the intensity of what they were dealing with, or the inevitability of choosing a husband at the end of this, but Rosalinde's heart had settled on *love* sometime during these last few days.

She didn't ask another question, didn't say another word. She wasn't sure she wanted to hear anything else about how Ombretta did or didn't feel about her father. It was strange thinking of him as a man with desires and feelings she couldn't understand, instead of just as her father. Part of her also felt guilty for talking to Ombretta about this, as if she was somehow betraying her mother, the woman King Tancred chose.

Ros was so caught up in her thoughts, she bumped into Ombretta when they stopped. "Sorry," she whispered, but Ombretta lifted her hand for silence. She pointed ahead of them and Rosalinde's eyes followed the path of her hand until they landed on a dark part of the forest that Ros would've overlooked if she hadn't been with them.

"Can you see it?" Ombretta asked.

"The shadowed place?" Ros asked.

Cassian said, "That's an illusion. Someone has made the area blend into the forest."

"What do you see?" Ros asked.

"I can see the illusion," Cassian said, "but I can see beyond it, too. It's hard to explain."

Ombretta asked, "Have you ever traced a picture? It's like that. You can see the picture you're drawing on top, but there's something underneath it that you can make out but it isn't as clear as the top layer."

"So the illusion is the top picture," Ros said. "Can we walk through it?"

Ombretta shook her head. "Not without being seen."

"Then how do we get in?"

Ombretta turned to her and smiled. "We're going to walk between the layers."

ROSALINDE FELT a chill roll down her spine as she looked between the illusion and the area she could now see. Every part of this felt unnatural. The illusion was to her left, shimmering with bright colors from this side of it. She felt heat rolling off it in waves.

Cool fingers of air tickled against her arms from the real forest on her right, or at least, what was left of it. There was a bare spot of ground singed black that looked as if fire had ravaged the land but had somehow been contained in a single, perfect ring. Nothing else about this place seemed strange and Ros wondered how many people had passed it without realizing there was anything unusual happening here.

"I don't see him," Cassian whispered.

"He's here," Ombretta said. "I don't know where, but I feel his presence."

Ros couldn't see or feel anything regarding Gaius from between the layers of real and illusion. She thought she might be able to, that some part of him had been left-over when the darkness had filled her and she had felt what it was like to be him, but perhaps not.

"What happens now?" she asked.

Cassian shrugged, but Ombretta said, "We can hide here for a while, but probably not long. He might already know we're here."

"There's no point in hiding," Cassian said. "Let's do what we came here to do."

Before Ombretta or Ros could reply, Cassian stepped through the layers into the blackened circle of the forest. Ros stared after him, her eyes transfixed on him as black electricity sparked all around him.

"He's okay. The Cradle is reacting to his magic, that's all," Ombretta breathed.

Ros wasn't sure which of them Ombretta's words were meant to comfort, but she didn't think it worked for either of them, as both of them stared after Cassian. He walked to the center of the ring and spun in a circle, his arms outstretched. "Gaius! Show yourself!"

Black mist rose from the ground, creeping around Cassian's ankles. It swirled together a few feet from him, coalescing into a black fog resembling the form of a man's shadow. Ros was almost certain she heard the semblance of a laugh coming from the darkness just before it rasped, "I wasn't sure you'd figure it out, hollow boy. You've always been a little slow."

"And you've always been a little cruel. Some things remain the same."

"Soft-hearted Cas. You'll never change, will you? I thought you might grow up a bit when you didn't have to linger in my shadow any longer, but I see that's not the case."

"Growing up and growing callous are different things, brother."

Gaius laughed again. "Spoken like the weakling you

are. Tell me, are you still suckling at Mother's teat, too? I know she's here, ready to spring out and protect her baby boy from his big bad brother."

Ombretta's hand grasped Rosalinde's wrist, her nails biting into the soft flesh, as she whispered, "Stay here. No matter what happens, you need to remain hidden, Your Highness."

And then she stepped out into the circle with her sons.

Ros watched her go, her insides quaking at the words Ombretta had spoken. There was a strange protectiveness in her tone that Ros hadn't expected. Perhaps it was for the king she once loved that she wanted to keep Ros safe, but her words contradicted the plan they'd put in place before they'd left Night house—the plan that involved all of them banding together as one.

"I'm here, my son," Ombretta said as she moved closer to Gaius.

"Well, well, well, the witch makes her appearance. I wasn't sure you were brave enough to face me, after everything you did."

Ombretta nodded. "I deserve your scorn, Gaius. I failed you. But your brother has done nothing wrong."

"He was born. That alone is an affront to me."

"Why?" Cassian asked. "You've hated me as long as I can remember, and I've never understood, since you were as necessary to me as the sun for a flower."

Gaius moved around the circle, adjusting his position so he wasn't stuck between Cassian and Ombretta. For a moment Ros was sure he wouldn't answer his brother, but then he said, "I didn't hate you at first. I wanted to be a good big brother, teach you about your gift and the world. But it became clear early on that you and I were meant to be rivals, not friends."

"I never felt that way," Cassian said.

"Because it isn't true," Ombretta said.

"Come now, Mother. You know what you did, setting us against one another."

"That was in your head—"

"No it wasn't!" he yelled, cutting her off. "You must've known what would happen when you were choosing our fathers, how we would differ, how your love for us would be different."

Ombretta shook her head. "I loved you both. You were different, yes, but that didn't change my love for you."

The bitterness in Gaius' tone was so thick it was nearly palpable. "You raised the darkness in me, Mother, but with him, you grew the light. There was never a doubt in my mind which of us you loved the most. But perhaps that's because you could never look at me without seeing King Tancred."

Ros felt her stomach drop to her feet. *No,* she thought. *It couldn't be. He couldn't mean...*

"I know you're out there, sis. I feel your blood reaching for me," Gaius said.

"She's not here," Ombretta lied.

The shadow-man ignored his mother's words,

speaking to Ros instead: "Do you feel it, Rosalinde? At your very core, you know I speak the truth."

"What are you talking about?" Cassian asked.

"She and I share a father. His Blood magic runs through both of us. Ask her, brother," Gaius said, turning to stare into the exact spot where Ros was hiding. He seemed to look through the illusion, his gaze meeting hers. "She knows."

And it was true. She wasn't sure how she didn't realize it before, how she didn't sense the same blood running through both of them. But now that she did, she couldn't deny it: Gaius was her half-brother, just as he was also Cassian's.

"Stings, doesn't it?" Gaius said. "To be fair though, my brother didn't realize he was pursuing my sister. Still, not appealing when you say it aloud."

"This can't be true," Cassian whispered.

Gaius responded gleefully, "But it is! I'm the throne's lost heir, and it's going to be one wild homecoming."

Twenty

◦◦◦

Despite Ombretta's warning, Rosalinde stepped through the layers and out into the Cradle. As soon as her foot touched the blackened earth, she gasped for breath. It felt like someone was squeezing the air from her lungs while holding her under water, drowning her with magic that didn't belong to her.

She scratched at her throat, fingers clawing at a force that wasn't there as she sucked in a thin trickle of air. Ros watched through watering eyes as Cassian and Ombretta exchanged confused glances, neither knowing what to do.

Ros fell to her knees and her vision started to go black at the edges. She felt a hand on her shoulder and a voice by her ear whispered, "Breathe, sister. Take in the Night magic. You belong here."

Ros shook her head. This place wasn't for her. She was a Water Elementalist.

"We share the same blood—blood that forms half of a Night mage's powers. Let go of what you think you're supposed to be and embrace the other powers that can be yours. Night magic is already in your blood. You can control it."

She fell forward, catching herself on her hands before her face hit the ground. She heard Cassian's voice, but it was from such a faraway place. Gaius, though, his voice was so close it might as well have been her own. "I can help you, but I'll have to leave a little of my essence attached to your body."

"No," she croaked. "Not again."

"You're going to die if I don't."

She heard the truth in his words. Though there was no reason to trust him after all that had happened, and she couldn't begin to understand why he wanted to help her, Ros still knew he was giving her the only option for survival.

"Do it," she mouthed.

Gaius cupped her cheek in his strange, shadow-hand. His thumb traced the corner of her lip and she felt a tiny part of the darkness seep into her mouth. Even in her rattled state, even knowing that he was her half-brother, and despite all that had happened when he'd tried to take control of her, this was still the most invasive thing that had ever happened to her. It was somehow worse than when he'd taken over her body before, but all she could think was that it was this, or die. Part of her wanted to choose the latter.

Her ragged breathing ceased. Air filled her lungs once more. Rosalinde's vision cleared and she could see the specks of long-dead embers clenched in her hands as she pushed herself up. As she stood, she looked at Cassian, Ombretta, and finally, Gaius.

Of all the things she had anticipated saying when she saw him, she surprised herself when she mouthed, "Thank you."

He nodded. "A one-time kindness, Princess. You'll get no further courtesy from me."

"Still, I'm grateful," she said.

Gaius stepped away from her then, edging toward the center of the circle as the others moved toward her. Cassian reached her first, putting his hands on her shoulders. "Are you okay?"

Ros nodded. "For now. But part of him..."

"I'm sorry," Ombretta said as she joined them. "I didn't anticipate the magic reacting like that."

"Why did it?" Cassian asked.

"Enough of this," Gaius said, drawing their attention. "You're here to defeat me, aye? Let's do it then."

Ombretta took a single step toward him, her face wearing the last bit of hope she had for her oldest son. "Gaius, please. It doesn't have to be like this. We can figure out a way to bring you back."

"Why would I want that? I was a weak, hurting husk

of a man. Now though, I'm powerful. Nothing holds me back."

"You need a body," Ros said, dredging up everything she knew of Gaius and his magic. "Without it, you're not at full power."

"There are plenty of bodies for the taking. Though if you're offering, yours fit rather well. Even better than Cassian's does."

"What are you talking about?" Cassian asked.

Gaius laughed. "I've hitched a ride on you a few times."

Cassian's brows quirked up. "When? Often?"

"Often enough. Haven't you noticed the shadows pooling when your anger rises?"

"That was you?"

"Sometimes," Gaius said. "I like coaxing the rage out of you. It's the only thing that proves we're family."

"We can find a way for you to have a body of your own. You won't have to rely on anyone else," Ombretta said.

"Whatever you're searching for, Ombretta, it isn't there. The part of me that was loyally devoted to you was sloughed away with my mortal flesh."

"I don't want your devotion, son. I want a relationship with you, a chance to love you. I want my son back."

Gaius threw his hands above his head and a black circle of smoke surrounded him, crackling with energy. "That sounds truly dreadful. I'd rather fight."

A spear of shadow shot from his hands. Ombretta

dived out of the way, but just barely. The shadow caught the edge of her cloak, ripping it to shreds.

He flung his other hand toward Cassian and dark tendrils slithered across the ground, faster than anything had any right to move. The shadow-snakes twisted around Cassian's legs and pulled him to the ground.

Ros looked at Gaius, horror clear in her expression. His face seemed brighter somehow, as if his violence brought him closer to life, transforming him from mere shadow. Ros shuddered. If he was willing to do this to his mother and brother, to try to *kill* them, what would he be willing to do to the rest of Talabrih if he had his chance? And, digging its claws deeper into her heart as she watched Cassian writhe against the shadows was another question: *what would become of Cassian?*

The thought sent fire through her blood. She would not let this *thing* hurt the man she loved. Ros reached for the magic inside her, flooding her senses with water and earth and power. She reached for the strength of her father and her mother, of her grandparents and those who came before them, of the long line of Elementalists whose powers had combined through the years to create everything she was.

And she *felt* them. She was no longer just a Water Elementalist with a proficiency in Tsunami; no, Rosalinde Adara Managold touched Fire and Air, Earth, and Water, and even Night. She wasn't a master of them like she was her own gift, but they were there if she needed them, tingling through her fingertips, begging to be used. She hoped the small part of Gaius left inside her couldn't feel what she was about to do.

"Gaius!" she yelled. "Stop this now."

His eyes shot up to hers, his lips curling in a sneer. "Stay out of this, little sister. I have no quarrel with you. At least, not today."

"Maybe not, but I have a quarrel with you. If you think I'm going to let you hurt them—"

"Let me?" he interrupted, the word coming out with a laugh. "I've felt your power, Princess. You may be strong elsewhere in comparison with the piddly mages who think they're noble, but you're in my domain now. In the Night's Cradle, you're helpless against me."

"We'll see about that," Ros said.

She flicked her wrists and flames shot up into her hand. There was a moment of confusion on Gaius' face before she released the fireballs at him. Ros treasured that second, relishing the surprise even as he jumped out of the fire's path. He landed on the ground a few feet from the shadowy circle that still hung in the air.

Gaius knelt, pressing his hands into the dark ring at his feet. Shadows began to pool around him, and Ros suddenly realized he hadn't *created* the ring of shadow suspended there, he was drawing from it.

Before the revelation could fully sink in, she called upon the powers of Earth house. She'd seen her mother weave flowers and trees from nothing, so she let her memories fuel the magic coming from her now. It pulled at the dirt and roots under the Cradle, the things that had been there long before magic had corrupted this place, the things that would remain long after this place was gone. Roots and grass pushed their way through the blackened earth, answering her call. They tangled around his legs and feet, holding him in place.

But the power of Earth house cannot hold a shadow and he slipped from its grasp like fingers trying to catch the breeze.

Gaius reappeared on her left, saying, "How are you doing that?"

The question surprised her. Not that he was curious, not that he was desperate to know, but that his voice was tinged with excitement. It was as if he was a child seeing magic for the first time.

"Please," he said, taking her pause as refusal to tell him. "I must know. I've never seen someone who could wield more than two gifts. I didn't think it was possible."

Ros ignored his words and instead pushed her hands toward him, releasing a gust of air. It wasn't strong like a real Air mage, but she could see the edges of his shadow body trailing away as the wind took hold, only to rejoin him after it passed.

"Impossible," he hissed.

But she was out of tricks now. He was right in saying her water wouldn't matter against him. Without calling it forth, she knew it might dissipate him for a moment like Air did, but it could do little more. There was only one thing left to do.

Ros sucked in a deep breath as she focused her

thoughts on her father. He was strong, his gift was powerful, and somehow, the Blood magic he used was tied to the Night. She let it build in her gut until it felt like her insides were boiling. When she called the dark into her hands, the blackness was tinged with blue, dancing in her hands like the flame had.

"No," he said. "I won't let you have this, too."

She felt that tiny sliver of him wriggle free of her body. Gaius smiled then, expecting the darkness to fall from her hands, expecting her to fall to the ground under the weight of the Cradle's magic as she had before. But she didn't fall and the magic didn't dissipate. He had taught her body how to survive in this place, whether he meant to or not, and now she could do it on her own.

Ros threw her hands forward and watched the shadow bolts fly toward him. He dodged one, knocked another out of the way. He hadn't seen her throw a third. It caught him square in the chest, the blue glow spreading out from the wound and taking over the darkness that formed him.

Gaius backed up, his steps no longer deliberate and sure. His eyes never left the spear in his chest and at first he didn't seem to notice he had stepped outside the Cradle's ring. He muttered, "This is nothing. I can fix this."

His gaze locked with Rosalinde's as confusion crossed his brow. Gaius looked down at his feet, realizing he'd left the protection of his power source. Just as he was about to step back into the ring, Ombretta threw herself into him instead. When they crashed together, his darkness seeped into her skin and the shadow boy that had been there only a moment before disappeared.

"What happened?" Ros asked.

"I've absorbed him," Ombretta said through gritted teeth. "But I don't know how long I can hold him."

"Release me," a voice crackled through her throat before she'd even finished her last sentence. Black smoke issued from her skin, thin and wispy, but escaping all the same.

"Let him go and we'll fight him together," Cassian said.

"No, I can't risk it. I lost one son already, I won't lose you, too."

"Mother, please," Cassian begged.

Ombretta's arm flew forward, a ball of shadow forming at her fingertips. Her face was contorted in pain as she struggled against Gaius and his control over her body. With one desperate attempt to save the others, Ombretta said, "Go."

She threw herself to the ground as her disobedient hand hurled the darkness at Ros. Ombretta's movement was enough to change the trajectory of the magic, though it barely missed. Cassian's arms were around her in an instant, pulling her through the bright colors of his teleportation and taking her away from the fight.

They appeared beside her bedroom window. The shadows in her room were thick and heavy, but they were nothing compared to the true darkness she had just seen.

Cassian's hands dropped from her and he said, "I have to go back."

"I can help you."

"No," he said. "I need you to be here, safe. But I have to see if I can rescue her. And maybe Gaius, too. I have to do this, even if there's only a slight chance I can do something."

"I know," she said, swallowing hard. She raised a hand to his cheek and whispered, "Be careful."

Cassian smirked. "Don't worry, Princess. I will always return for you."

Tears sprang to Rosalinde's eyes unbidden. There was so much still unsaid and no time to say it. There was one thing more important than anything else and she needed him to know. "Cassian, I lo—"

But he was gone.

She stood in her empty bedroom, her heart pounding, and she whispered into the darkness, "I love you."

Twenty-One

Rosalinde stood from the tub and let droplets trail down her body. The foaming, scented water was filthy now, removing every trace of her time in the forest.

Still, she couldn't forget. The darkness. The surge of power. The hurt on Cassian's face, the resolve in Ombretta's eyes, when they faced Gaius. Rosalinde shivered. She couldn't forget now, and she never would.

Ros stepped on the plush carpet beside the basin and wrapped a robe around herself. She padded into the bedroom to get ready for the choosing ceremony. When she'd gone to speak with her mother last night, she wasn't sure there would be a ceremony today. Her father was still missing and she was back to square one.

Queen Sariyah was devastated that the king hadn't been found. As she listened to all that had happened, she grew quiet, pensive even. When Ros finished her tale, the queen straightened her hands across her dress and swallowed hard. "We can send another party to search for your father, but as tomorrow is the seventh day, we cannot delay having you choose your husband. The ceremony will commence on schedule."

"Mother, there is more going on here—"

"I know," she said. "That's why we must proceed with caution. You will become the new ruler, my darling, and we need to make sure that happens before the other shoe drops."

"Then you see it, too. These things are all connected."

"I see it, but I don't know who is behind it."

"I'd wager it's someone from Air."

Sariyah shrugged. "Maybe. Hessian Barclay has never hidden his desire for the throne. But just because he's the obvious choice doesn't mean he's the only one. We need to be careful."

Ros nodded. "I'll do my part. Maybe we'll have more information once the ceremony is over and we can figure out a new plan."

"Speaking of the ceremony," Sariyah asked, eyeing her daughter, "do you know who you're going to choose?"

"I do."

Her mother smiled. "Is it a certain dashing Night mage?"

Ros grinned. "Perhaps."

Sariyah took her hand. "If he is the one you want, I

will support any decision you make. I trust your judgment."

"He's the one I want," Ros had whispered to her mother.

She whispered it again now as she sat on her bed staring through the open window. There was no doubt in her head or her heart that Cassian was the right choice.

Ros pulled the last of her clothes on and stood to go to the vanity table, but something on her pillow caught her eye. She reached over and picked up the folded piece of paper. It was sealed with an upside-down triangle with a line through it pressed into green wax—the elemental symbol for Earth.

She smiled. Probably something silly from Larkin meant to calm her nerves before she chose her husband. She broke the seal and opened the paper. She recognized her best friend's handwriting immediately and quickly read the single sentence upon it. Then she read it again. And again. The words started to blur together and she realized she was crying.

One sentence, each word a punch to the gut.

She jolted when someone knocked on the door. A servant called, "Princess, they're waiting for you."

Ros wasn't sure how long she'd been sitting there staring at the paper, or when she'd fallen to her knees beside her bed. She called back, "I'll be right there."

She stood and folded the paper, tucking it away in the hidden pocket of her dress. Though it was out of sight, the words still danced before her eyes:

If you want to see your father alive again, choose Earth.

Ros tried not to look for Larkin when she entered the throne room, but the girl stood out like the only green tree in a forest of gray. She was gorgeous, as usual, in a floor-length gown dotted with tiny emeralds that glittered in the light streaming through the tall windows. Her *best friend* stood beside her brother—the jerk had the nerve to smile at her—and their parents were behind them talking to a noble from Fire house. The sight of them all made Rosalinde's skin crawl, while the knowledge of what Larkin and Zandor had done made her feel like she was going to vomit.

It took Ros a moment to calm her stomach and her nerves as she walked down the center of the room toward the dais. Her mother and sister stood to either side of the throne; oblivious to the turmoil in Ros as she walked toward them, they stood statuesque and resplendent in matching scarlet gowns cut to fit like gloves. She envied them a bit, even now while she was the center of attention. Their grace was easy, perfectly suited to the royal family—meanwhile Ros could barely walk through the court because her knees were wobbling so badly.

She looked at the chair they stood beside, her father's empty throne. Ros steeled herself against the pang of guilt and hurt ricocheting through her gut as she marched toward it. They expected her to sit there, to make her pronouncement from the throne and become their new ruler in King Tancred's absence, but she knew she couldn't do it. Sitting there felt like betrayal, and she'd had enough of that already.

Ros stepped onto the dais, her black gown swishing as she climbed the steps. She gave her family a smile before turning to face the assembly. She wasn't ready to see Cassian; part of her hoped she wouldn't have to see him, unsure she'd have the willpower to do what she must with him there.

But of course, there he was, front and center. He wore his customary black, and she hoped he took notice of the dress she'd chosen to match him. For the first time, she wished he could read her mind and understand that she was doing what she had to, not what she wanted to. She looked into his eyes and wished for a lot of things.

When he smiled up at her, the hope beaming from his face brighter than the sun, it almost broke her resolve. She wanted to call him forward, name him as her betrothed, and let him know exactly how she felt.

She took a deep breath and let her eyes move from him to wander over the rest of the crowd. Teague and Beckett stood at the back of the room, sharing a secret smile; William was seated beside Graeme at the front of the assembly as they recovered from their wounds; she saw Florian with his cousin, and when their eyes met, he nodded at Cassian and gave her a thumb's up.

It was all she could do not to break down right then,

reliving all she had done over the last few days. Everything had been for naught.

Instead, she turned her gaze to the room and let her eyes bore into Larkin's. Ros said, "I've known the end of this story since I was a child. The Princess chooses her husband, chooses the future king for Talabrih. Little did I know, there was never really a choice for me."

Whispers cascaded through the room at her words, unsure what to make of them. She lifted her hands to silence them, saying, "I have met some wonderful men through this journey and I hope we can continue to work together for the future of our land, even though I'm unable to choose you to walk this path with me." She took a deep breath, her eyes flicking to Cassian one last time before she said the thing that would change everything.

"Love can take you by surprise and make your world a brighter place. That's what happened to me throughout this last week. I had no idea the revelation in store for me when the Great Match began.

"But some of you did," she said, letting her gaze return to the Earth house nobles. "Some of you knew that I'd never considered *him* as a mate, though I've known him all my life. But my eyes have been opened to exactly who he is, and exactly what kind of king he would be. So please, welcome my fiancé to the dais: Lyzandor Zolto of Earth house."

A polite smattering of applause echoed through the room, though Ros was certain the stunned silence was far louder. Zandor himself looked surprised when his name was called, as if he hadn't had a hand in this whole charade.

Ros glanced to Cassian—or where he had been. But he was gone. Disappeared like only a Night mage could.

She wanted to believe she could track him down and tell him the truth about what was happening, but she knew it was just a pretty lie she was telling herself. Even if she could find him—which she had no idea where to start looking—and if he would listen and maybe even help her, Cassian wasn't interested in being second. Her heart was divided between loving him and saving her father, but Cassian wanted all or nothing. He wouldn't accept the trade she made to rescue King Tancred, even if he understood why she did it.

Zandor was beside her now, one hand slipping around her waist as he waved to the crowd. Behind them, Queen Sariyah said, "It is an honor to welcome you to the family, Lyzandor Zolto. We will make plans for the wedding and send out invitations in the near future. Congratulations to Earth house for raising this esteemed Elementalist and your future king!"

The clapping was louder this time, though Rosalinde didn't believe there was sincerity to it. Whether it was because the other houses were disappointed about not getting their own competitor in, or because they all lacked enthusiasm where Zandor was concerned, Ros couldn't say. He'd always been a quiet boy living on the outside of the other nobles' lives, and none seemed to know what to make of the man who stood before them now—the man who would be king.

As the applause faded, Elsabet chimed in, "Since we have competitors returning in three months for the alternate Great Match that's been arranged, perhaps we should have the royal wedding then? It would be a beautiful way to celebrate the new couples who find one another through matches of their own."

Queen Sariyah's eyes narrowed slightly as she said, "Lovely idea, but of course it will be at the discretion of Princess Rosalinde. I'm certain she's eager to begin her life with—"

"Three months is fine," Ros said, cutting her off. "It shall be done at the new Match."

She wanted to throw her arms around Elsa and smother her in kisses. Her sister had bought her three whole months to find a way out of this arrangement. It wasn't a long time, but weddings from the Great Match usually fell anywhere from a week to a month after. Three months was unheard of. Ros wouldn't have thought of such a thing herself, but having her sister say it in front of the whole assembly gave her the perfect excuse for the delay.

Ros turned and forced a smile at her betrothed. His brows furrowed for only a second at the mention of the delay before his face smoothed out and he said, "As you wish, my love."

"Wonderful," Queen Sariyah said. "Now that everything is settled, let's retire to the dining hall for a celebratory feast."

"Certainly, Your Majesty," Rosalinde said, "but isn't there one thing you're forgetting?"

Sariyah's face paled at her daughter's words, though it had been her idea to do the choosing ceremony and the coronation at the same time. Perhaps the sudden change in Rosalinde's choices had startled her. Sariyah asked, "And what's that, darling?"

"It's time to make me queen."

Twenty-Two

The crowning was not a grand affair. Maybe it would have been, if Rosalinde had allowed for the time needed to prepare. But in truth, she didn't care about all that. She didn't want the throne and had no desire to be queen, not when everything around her seemed to be falling apart. Still, she did it because it was the smart thing to do.

Anything could happen between now and her wedding, and there was a chance she wouldn't find her father, especially now that she didn't have Cassian's help. Better she take the throne now and foil any other plans that might be underway, rather than wait and let Earth house have another chance to steal their way onto it.

The impartial judges who had graded the contestants at the opening ceremony were called forth, each reciting their house's oath of loyalty to the new ruler. The nobles present did their parts, clapping or reciting when they were supposed to, silent the rest of the time. She wasn't sure if it was supposed to be that way or if they were in shock. Ros had never seen the crowning ceremony herself, but something about this still felt mild in comparison to what she'd imagined.

It wasn't until Queen Sariyah removed the crown from her own head and placed it on her daughter's that the whole thing became real to Rosalinde. Until then, it had seemed tactical, the best move in this strange game she was playing. When the crown rested on her brow, she became fully aware of the weight of it. She was Talabrih's ruler now. Everything she did would impact her kingdom.

But maybe, with a lot of planning and a little luck, she could make more of this than her enemies imagined. She wasn't the same girl they knew from a week ago. She was stronger, braver, and though she was broken at this moment, she wouldn't stay that way. Rosalinde was the Queen of Talabrih, and with help or alone, she would figure out a way to get what she wanted.

Whatever the cost.

Afterword

Thank you for reading *The Fall of Water House.* I hope you enjoyed the beginning of Rosalinde's adventure! If you did, please leave me a review, stop by my website, or find me on social media. I'd love to hear from you. You all mean the world to me and I'm truly thankful for the time you've given my book.

If you'd like to try another story with royals, magic, and new book boyfriends, check out my mermaid series starting with *Black Sea Bright Song*.

You may also like my sci-fi series under Shelly Jarvis: The Book of the Golden One duology starts with *The Dreamwalker* or the 3-book post apocalyptic series Little Star begins with *Even Ghosts Have Teeth*.

About the Author

Michelle Jarvis is a fantasy romance author with a penchant for royalty. She loves diverse characters and believes everyone deserves a love story.

While Michelle has had her own love affair with writing since she was in elementary school, it wasn't until her late thirties that she realized how much fun it was to turn up those romantic subplots. Now she's combining her love of fantasy and her newfound passion for romance to put them into the hands of readers.

Michelle lives in West Virginia with her partner and their rescue dogs–Gimli, Pickles, and Fergus–as well as Ethel Furman the bunny who also thinks she's a dog.

For free books, bonus scenes, and news about upcoming releases, sign up for Michelle's mailing list on her website: www.authormichelle.com

www.ingramcontent.com/pod-product-compliance
Lightning Source LLC
Chambersburg PA
CBHW050714180626
46814CB00002B/437